Dime Novel Suitor

Dime Novel Suitor

By
Carrie Fancett Pagels

Hearts Overcoming Press

This book is a work of fiction. Names, characters, places, and incidents are either products of the author's imagination or used fictitiously.

ISBN: 979-8-9928267-3-9

Hearts Overcoming Press
Printed in the United States of America.
All rights reserved

Cover Art by: Stephanie Anderson, *Book Designer*, Alt 19 Creative

Originally published in: *Seven Brides for Seven Mail-Order Husbands* Collection from Barbour Publishing

Dedication

To:

Joan Carol Belsky Pagels and Donald R. Pagels
Thanks for supporting your daughter-in-law's writing!

Chapter One

Turtle Creek, Kansas, April 1866

*P*a *had some kind of nerve up and dying like that—just when I'd gotten used to Frank being gone.* Adjusting her faded black crape bonnet, Caroline Kane exited what was now her inn, onto the boardwalk and then stepped down to the hard-packed dirt street. She needed to visit her parents' graves before the busy day began. As she waited for the dairy wagon, young Jake Miller waved as he drove past. Would his widowed mother find a husband in the upcoming auditions? What a hare-brained notion. Mrs. Miller sure could use extra help, though, that a husband would provide.

As for Caroline, she was fine. Perfectly fine.

"We'll manage just fine," she mumbled to herself.

"Caroline!"

Caroline pivoted to spy Mrs. Reed emerging from the alley alongside the Tumbleston Inn. The older woman shuffled toward her, bent forward as usual, rubbing her gnarled hands.

"What are you doing up so early, Mrs. Reed?"

"I wish you'd just call me, Mae, child." She lifted her chin, and her pale blue eyes glimmered.

"Doesn't seem natural, ma'am, but I'll try." She smiled at the widow, who'd only recently joined the inn's staff. "So you're an early bird today, too?"

The worry over all the incoming men to the inn had Caroline tossing and turning. Not only would she have to put the men up but they'd have to feed them and somehow she'd have to keep her two younger sisters from being accosted by any of them.

Mae cringed. "Couldn't sleep. My rheumatism predicts a storm coming." The silver-haired widow flexed open her right hand and grasped her left one, massaging the swollen knuckles. "Wanted to ask if you believe we've enough biscuits put aside for this morning?"

"Deanna did the count last night before she went to sleep." Caroline sighed. "I hate to serve cold biscuits, but with Pa gone I'm still trying to figure out how to make everything work."

"We'll get help. The Lord never fails us." Mae turned to go back to the inn.

A gust of breeze ruffled Caroline's dark skirts as she crossed the street and headed south, past the Town Green and on toward the beckoning field behind the church. Rosy glow hovered over the far treeline as the sun determined to rise, despite all that had happened. Life would go on, regardless. She swiped her wet face, and continued on toward the cemetery, her laced boots chafing at her heels.

He's not there. Caroline stopped. Pa was in heaven now, albeit all too soon, like Frank. '*Every day is a precious gift*,' Pa had often said. With her mother deceased now these past five years, and Frank gone two, Caroline was truly alone.

Alone?

Caroline drew in a deep breath of fresh morning air, full of the promise of rain. With five younger siblings, an interfering older sister, plus an inn filled with Turtle Creek's cast-offs as workers, she was hardly alone.

But with her feelings cracked open like eggs ready to be scrambled, she'd never felt lonelier.

Kansas City
How ironic that Barden Granville's first foray into the world of cowboys was in an establishment called "The Empire" with its overdone velvet and damask upholstery and wallpaper a laughable imitation of the grand salons of Europe. His older

brother, who would inherit the title of Earl, and Cheatham estate, would have referred to the décor as "Agony in Red" with all the vermillion in the room. Blue smoke hung overhead like a dark cloud in the crowded tavern. Barden coughed as yet another of the cowboys at his card table lit up a cigar.

Chairs scraping the filthy wooden floor competed with the noise of the serving girls' laughter. Some of the scantily clad young women were no older than his youngest sister. The clergyman within him yearned to take the girls aside and inquire whether they understood what a slippery slope they traversed.

The pock-marked youth adjacent to him threw down a coin. "Who'll match me?"

Barden surreptitiously examined his cards as the other men either folded their cards or plucked a coin from pockets grimed with road dirt. He placed his wager, a niggling of guilt convicting him that this was a bad idea.

When the cards were all spread atop the table, the stunning realization hit him. "Criminy, I won!"

The largest of the men, with silver edging his temples, pushed his pile of silver coins toward Barden. The other men glanced at the older man first before slowly sliding their money across the table.

The man with the filthy red bandana around his thick neck squinted at Barden. "We'll see who wins next time."

None of the men had shared their names. Maybe cowboys didn't.

As a waitress passed, one of the men flung out an arm and tugged her closer. "Stop that!" She slapped at his hand.

Barden pushed his chair back. "I say, unhand her."

"Or you'll do what?"

He was an excellent pugilist, although his father would have chucked Barden from the house had he known he'd taken up bare knuckle fighting while at Oxford. "I fear I'd have to teach you a lesson."

Laughter erupted. The men mocked his words, repeating them with an exaggerated British accent making him sound like a fop. His opponents could confirm he was no such thing, had they been present—which they were not.

The silver-haired man shoved the table over. Barden's fists took on a life of their own as shouts and screams ensued.

Then Barden descended into darkness.

Head pounding in agony, Barden lay against dank earth that seeped moisture through his clothing. He blinked up at a pale blue sky tinged with golden light. Sunrise. He pressed his eyelids closed. *Where am I exactly?* Brick walls flanked him left and right. A brass band playing American tunes seemed to have occupied his brain. He pressed his eyes closed, which helped quiet the noise in his head.

A door slammed shut nearby and Barden flinched.

Quick footsteps neared. "Lawd have mercy. You all right?" Compassion tinged the woman's words, making him all the sorrier for his plight.

A groan was all he could manage.

"Oh my." She gasped. "I be right back."

The woman hurried off. Barden tried to move, but every body part screamed in agony. Slowly, he flexed his feet. Those cowboys had stolen his new boots. He never should have sat down with them at the card table.

If this was his dream come true, then what would a nightmare be like? *Oh, Lord, sovereign God, why me? Why now? I've waited all my life for this. Am I being punished?* Was it for being an ungrateful third son who would never inherit?

Barden bent his knees. There was something to be grateful for—his legs still worked. At least they could bend. He tried to raise his head, but everything seemed to spin. When he dropped his head back onto the dirt, the stench of alley odors suddenly predominated. He'd been tossed in a back alley like refuse.

The door slammed again and quick heavy footsteps thudded toward him. "He gonna need a doctor, Uziah."

"I'll go get him." The man's deep voice seemed to rumble from his chest.

"First help me get him inside."

"But where we gonna put him, Mary?" The affection in his voice suggested this woman was special to him. *His wife?*

"That little alcove in the kitchen." Mary pressed a hand to Barden's head. "Go and put that pallet down on the floor, Uziah, and come back out and help me."

Soon, Barden found himself laid out on a thin mattress, covered with a threadbare blanket.

Before he could say, "Thank you," he slumbered.

Looking up from her dishwashing, Caroline dried her hands on her apron and glared at her older sister. "You forgot to tell me *what*?"

Lorraine batted her blonde eyelashes. "I contributed to the mail-order husband ad."

"Are you out of your cotton-picking mind?" Caroline raised her hands. "You're already married."

"For you, you ninny! Now that you seem to realize Frank is gone." Lorraine's words slapped her.

Caroline could only stare, gape-mouthed. Only since Pa's death had she truly accepted that she was a widow.

"Well, aren't you going to thank me?"

"No!"

Alvin looked up from where he sat, by the door, peeling potatoes. Their seventeen-year-old brother smirked. "How's it feel having other people making decisions for you?"

"Just hush, Al!" Caroline glared at him. Would the seventeen-year-old still be alive had their father allowed him to go fight in the war?

Picking up a torn dish towel, Lorraine tut-tutted. "Ma would never have let the inn get so run down like Pa did." *Or like Caroline, was the inference.*

"You don't even live here and Pa left the inn to me, so you've no need to bother yourself." Caroline yanked the stained cloth from her sister. "What are you doing by going behind my back and putting my name in on that husband auditioning thing?"

"You'll thank me later."

"I won't do it."

"Then I'll pick someone for you." Lorraine's smirk promised that she would. "Trust me, Caroline, you'll be happy once the inn starts making money from new customers in town for the husband auditions." She averted her gaze and picked at her lace cuffs. "On that note, I should mention I volunteered for the auditions to be held here. In the dining hall."

"What!" Both Caroline and Alvin shouted at the same time.

When her younger brother jumped up from his chair, Caroline held out a staying hand. "Lorraine, you had no right!"

"They'll pay well for the privilege of using the restaurant from four to six that afternoon."

"And will expect food, no doubt."

Twin circles of red appeared on her sister's fair cheeks. "Yes. But something simple."

"Well, I'm not going to be participating and I'll not even be here. . ." Not that she now realized her interfering sister had gone in on the ad, in Caroline's name. "So you'd better figure out a way to serve them."

Her sister merely shrugged.

If Caroline were ten years younger she'd be rolling around on the floor with Lorraine like they used to do when her older sister would try to hide her Jane Austen novels. "Did it not occur to you that we'll have to serve an evening meal to our guests, too?"

"Pooh! Most of the men will be staying here. If they are full up on sandwiches, cookies, punch and coffee, you can give them stew and biscuits for dinner."

She would have argued, but that rationale actually made sense. "I don't want Deanna or Virginia involved in this either. I don't need any of those men thinking they're looking for husbands."

"I'm much happier married and I know you would be, too, if only you'd open yourself up again to the possibility."

"Wonderful! Then you and Joel can take Henry and Leonard in at your ranch and share your happiness with them—

like you first promised Pa." Then reneged on the promise as he drew closer to death.

Eyes widening, Lorraine opened her reticule. "That reminds me! I just got a letter from Grandmother."

"Grandmother Tyler?" Pa's people had died in South Carolina years earlier. Ma's folks in Virginia were too prideful to associate with them.

"Yes. Grandmother Tyler."

"What?"

"Just read it." Lorraine shoved the cream-colored missive at Caroline. "I have to run. Need to see the milliner about my new hat."

Caroline didn't bother to wave goodbye as her sister fled with her usual rapidity. Lorraine was good at running away from conflict. That was how she'd become Mrs. Martinchek.

"What are you gonna do?" Alvin set another peeled potato into the crockery bowl. "We could use the extra money and I'm willing to help. Henry and Leonard can help, too."

Caroline pulled a stool out from beneath the work counter and sat down. "She makes me so angry. Lorraine has no right to interfere."

"Kinda hurt us boys' feelings when she wouldn't let us come out to the ranch."

"Yes, well. . ." She didn't need sensitive Alvin dwelling on these thoughts. "She's newly married."

Entering from the dining room, Mrs. Reed waved an empty bread basket. "Our guests are awfully hungry this morning."

What would they do when the men arrived for the auditions? Surely many would cram into every available space at the inn. They'd be working around the clock.

Caroline needed help—and fast.

Chapter Two

Kansas City, May, 1866

*B*arden raised his hands from the dishwater and examined them. At least he no longer possessed the soft palms and fingers with which he'd begun this journey. Mary Freeman entered the kitchen, shaking her head.

"Sorry, Bard. No telegrams at the office."

He swiveled to face her. "I sent something to every one of my Father's British rancher friends in all the surrounding area." No answers, though. Time had come for Barden to move on.

Uziah joined them. "Need me some more coffee."

Barden pointed to the pot on the stove. "Brewed up another before I started on these dishes."

Mary beamed her approval. Her husband poured himself a mug of the stuff that Bard had come to enjoy even more than a cup of good English tea in the morning.

Raising the mug to his lips, Uziah hesitated but then drank some. "Good." He drank some more, turned, his white teeth showing in his big smile. "You done real good."

"Thank you, Mr. Freeman."

Mary and her husband exchanged a look. "Our friend, Mr. Tumbleston, send word to us this past winter, that they needed help at his inn. He's passed on, Lord rest his soul, but I reckon his daughter, Mrs. Kane, would take you on."

Yes, it was time.

"Mrs. Kane helped us out when we first arrived in Kansas and we'll always be grateful. I'd sure like to return the favor."

"I reckon you competent to give her some relief, now you learned the ropes." Uziah had given Barden a true compliment.

"Thank you, sir." Competent wasn't a word he'd often heard ascribed to himself, other than at seminary.

At his family's estate, he'd always been the ignored third brother. But his valet recognized Barden's proficiency in reading and had supplied boxes of American dime novels. Through that paperback tutelage, Barden realized he'd been born on the wrong continent. Before he settled down into his ministry in pastoral northern England, he'd live the cowboy life. Although how he'd do that at an inn, he didn't know.

Two days later, traveling across Kansas, his back ached worse than any hunt he'd been on, riding and jumping over hill and dale in chase of an elusive fox. And his stop at the Martinchek's ranch failed to procure Barden a spot as a hand. The rest of the drive into Turtle Creek was a blur of green, as he silently vented at God for His failure to help him in his quest to enjoy cowboy life, even if for only a few months.

The drayman pulled to the side of the street, by a painfully plain building, much like one back home in England—a large ordinary in Leeds. The Tumble Inn, a white-washed wooden structure, stood three stories high, as did few others in this small borough. No shutters, no protective portico, nothing decorative on the front. The windows bore evidence of street grime, failing to reflect back the sun's impressive glare. Still, he wasn't here to pass judgment.

Barden grabbed his bag and hopped down. Although he had few coins to spare, he pulled one from his pocket and offered it.

The driver shook his head. "No, sir, Uziah pay me good to get you here."

"Well then. . ." Barden tucked the coin back in his vest pocket. "Thank you."

"I can't be lingerin'. God go with you." The man's soulful eyes were gentle unlike his father's accusatory ones.

If Father knew he was here. . . This wasn't how Barden had planned to spend his American holiday. He was supposed to be on a ranch, enjoying a bit of cowboy life before settling into the remote northern village that was to be his home and into a stone-walled vicarage that could have fit into this inn several times over.

Couples emerged from the inn, chatting, followed by some solitary men and women. A middle-aged woman attired in a sapphire blue damask dress held fast to the arm of a red-haired man whose smile could not have been any broader.

Love was a beautiful thing, regardless of age. Too bad those young women interested in him had viewed him only as Lord Cheatham's third son, one who'd inherit nothing.

The front double doors were centered in the inn. Choosing the brass handle on the right, he held fast, hesitating. Should he go around to the back? Like the common servant he'd become?

Before he could choose, the door opened out on him, propelling him backward. He'd almost lost his footing, but recovered, a credit to his Cotillion dance instructor no doubt.

A beautiful young woman, with glossy reddish-brown hair coiled atop her head, frowned at him. Her flashing brown eyes surveyed him from head to toe. "The auditions are over. The restaurant is closed while we prepare dinner."

He raised his hands. "Auditions?"

Turtle Creek was, indeed, an unusual place. He should pull out his glasses so he could clearly read what was pasted to the door, but before he could do so, the pretty Kansan swiveled away and yanked the placard from it.

"Darned nuisance."

"Pardon me, I'm. . ."

"You're not here for a room, are you?" She crossed her arms over her black bombazine-covered chest.

"No, I fear not, Miss. . ."

Her chin lifted slightly, and her winsome features relaxed, but she didn't offer her name.

Barden cleared his throat. "I'm here for Mrs. Caroline Kane."

She eyed him warily. "Why?"

Was this Mrs. Kane? "I'm answering the advertisement."

"Well, you're a bit late."

Uziah and Mary had said the inn owner needed assistance as had the Martinchek ranch owners, where he'd stopped outside of town. Barden's bag seemed to grow heavier. What would he do if he found no work here?

"Did my sister send you?"

Was Mrs. Martinchek her sister? He couldn't remember the Freemans saying so. "Looks very much like you, only a less vibrant version?" He'd spoken briefly with the owner's wife, just as he was leaving the Martinchek ranch. She'd just arrived home, and looked to be in a huff. But she had spoken with him briefly, encouraging him to seek out Mrs. Kane.

Guilt assailed Caroline at the flutters this stranger was bringing to her bruised heart. His delightful British accent was one Caroline had dreamed of when she'd read her mother's stash of Jane Austen novels. And now he seemed to indicate he considered her to be the prettier sister, not Lorraine. She'd even overheard Frank confess that he considered her older sister to be loveliest of all the girls in town. Caroline ran her fingers along her buttoned up collar, which suddenly felt too tight.

Would Lorraine carry through with her threat that if Caroline wouldn't pick a suitor from the auction that she'd pick one for her?

"So someone sent you over here then?"

"Yes." He averted his gaze. The sun illuminated the gold in his dark blond hair, but his gray eyes were what caught her attention. They were so clear, and fathomless as the deepest of still waters.

Exhaling in a whoosh, Caroline gestured to the side of the building. "Let's go around to the bench and talk about this."

"Indeed."

He offered his arm to her. Caroline pulled back, surprised by the gesture. The last time she'd linked her arm with a man's had been when Frank and she walked down the main street for a final goodbye before he was to leave for war. When the man kept his arm extended, she gently rested her fingers atop his flannel-covered arm. Beneath the cloth she felt the sinewy strength of his muscles. He led her toward the wrought iron bench, a gift shipped from back east to her mother years earlier. They sat, each at the corner of the seat, angled in toward one another.

"What's your name?" Would he have a dreadful last name that she'd have to take, if she caved in to Lorraine's wishes?

"My pardons. Barden Granville the. . ." He clamped his mouth shut.

"Are you ashamed to admit your profession?" What type of job was he not wanting to admit to? Or was it some characteristic? Barden the criminal? From what she'd seen of the "audition men" who were staying at the inn, a few seemed to be ne'er do wells.

Mr. Granville rubbed his hand over his chin. "I most recently have been working as a chef, well as a cook rather, at an establishment in Kansas City."

"I see." She couldn't help smiling. This could be promising. If he really could cook. "Are you a sober man?"

His eyebrows rose. "Other than Eucharist wine, I don't partake."

"Good. And since you mention communion, I assume you are a Christian."

Eyelashes a tad too thick for a man closed over his pale eyes for a long moment, almost as though he was praying. "I am."

This man was too good to be true. But Caroline wasn't about to jump into a marriage with a complete stranger. Frank and she had grown up together. But he'd not made her stomach do the strange things it was doing now. Maybe it was the punch. She smoothed out some creases in her dress.

"I fear I've taken you by surprise, Mrs. Kane. Please accept my apologies for arriving after the auditions." His rich baritone voice warmed her.

Her sister must have coached this man in his lovely, but fake, British accent knowing that would appeal to Caroline. But she'd find out. Give it time and the truth revealed itself. "You're here now, and we'll see what needs to be done."

"It has been my every intention to aid you in any conceivable way that I might." He nibbled his lower lip and frowned.

Was he lying about something?

"What exactly do you mean?"

"I spent some time working at the Freemans' place."

"With Mary and Uziah?" Such good people.

"Yes. They are well and send their greetings." When he grinned, an adorable dimple formed in one cheek.

She mustn't stare. "Well, good. I haven't laid eyes on them in far too long."

"If I say so, myself, I've become a jolly good cook under their tutelage."

Who spoke like that? "How long have you been in America?"

"Not long."

That could be a good thing, because if he became homesick for British soil then Caroline could in good conscience send him packing. Something about him fascinated her, and had her breath seemingly stuck in her throat.

"Fortunately the Freemans took me in when I came upon some misfortune.

Oh no, was this some kind of song and dance he did? Was Barden a swindler? But Mary and Uziah wouldn't have sent him on if he was.

"Both send their condolences as well." His voice dropped and held genuine sympathy.

Caroline blinked back unshed tears. "Well, then."

Goodness, the ladies must have paid a pretty penny to even place an advertisement in Kansas City. For Mary and Uziah to have seen the husband auditions ad, and then thought of Caroline, touched her. They must have thought highly of this man – if he was telling the truth. She'd send them a missive to find out. But she had her sisters and brothers to protect, too. She mustn't let her hammering heart direct her brain. "Let me tell you how this will work."

"Pray do." His lips twitched. From the way he sat erect at the end of the bench, Mr. Granville reminded her of one of those portraits of Lords of the manor. But this wasn't his manor. This was her inn.

"How do you feel about sharing responsibility for my five siblings? Granted, they aren't young children, but they do yet require oversight."

His features tugged in puzzlement. "I will certainly pitch in. Mary didn't mention them."

"I would think that would be rather important in you making your decision." And why had he claimed to not be there for the auditions. Puzzling. But likely Joel had told him he was too late and then her sister probably jumped on the chance to send Mr. Granville their way. How triumphant she must be feeling at this moment.

"It doesn't deter me in the slightest." He beamed in such an angelic way, she believed him.

"And there will be no decisions made until at least six weeks have passed." She wasn't about to jump into marriage with a stranger, even if he was handsome and spoke with an accent that sent thrills through her. Not even if he had clear gray eyes that one could disappear into. Not even if that dimple near his perfect lips was completely adorable. Not even if he might chase off the memories of her beloved Frank.

"That suits me fine, Mrs. Kane."

Mrs. Kane. The way he said her name, so stiffly, certainly didn't imply any lascivious intent, but she should make things clear. "You'll have a room on the top floor. You'll not reference yourself as anything other than our hired man."

She would not be made a laughingstock. She'd said she wouldn't audition a man for husband and she hadn't. *Then what do you call this?*

"Of course." His brows drew together, forming a line on his smooth brow.

He was taking things well. A good sign for a potential spouse. Perhaps there was hope after all. Frank hadn't been malleable at all. He'd always been the kind of boy who would do exactly what he wanted, when he wanted.

"I need the most help with dinner. Especially with all the men here in town for the auditions and the coach now stopping here more frequently."

"Glad to be of service, Mrs. Kane."

His voice was softer this time and he leaned toward her.

How would *Mrs. Granville* sound on his lips? Her cheeks heated at the thought. "I could use a hand with the wood throughout the day, keeping the stove going, too."

"I am at your beck and call." He raised his hands as though in surrender and smiled in a slow satisfied way, his eyelids slipping to half closed.

Caroline's heartbeat raced. No man had ever had this effect upon her, not even her husband. She stood and wiped at her skirt. "Follow me and I'll show you to your room."

Before he could respond, she turned on her heel and headed to the back entrance.

Lord, I don't know what you're up to, but it better be good.

She chewed her lower lip. *Sorry, Lord, I know that's disrespectful. I sure could use a break, though, and soon. Thank you for what You are already doing in my life.*

Chapter Three

*B*arden followed Mrs. Kane's shapely form up narrow stairs for two flights, stopping at a dusting landing with cobweb strewn windows at each end. "Don't the cleaning girls tidy up on this floor?" Nor on the other landings, as far as he could see.

"Mrs. Reed isn't able to reach that high, nor is Mr. Woodson." She didn't offer to explain who Mrs. Reed or Mr. Woodson were.

Barden trailed her down the stuffy hall. First chance he had, he'd open the windows to allow in fresh air.

A scream erupted from down the hall. "Give that back!" A chestnut-haired youth ran down the corridor toward them clutching a stuffed rabbit and laughing.

"Stop!" Mrs. Kane expertly snatched the toy from the miscreant's hands.

"Pa gave me that!" A young lady dressed in a coffee-colored calico dress covered with a white ruffled pinafore, raced toward them, her light brown braid bobbing against her back. "I'm going to kill him if he does that again."

Barden stepped between the boy and girl. "No, you shan't. The Lord frowns upon murder."

The dark-haired youth came alongside Mrs. Kane. "You a preacher, mister?"

Before Barden could reply, his new employer shook her head. "No, Leonard. He's our new—"

"Did you get him at the auction, Sis?" The green-eyed young lady grinned up at Barden.

"No! And it wasn't an auction, Deanna. You make it sound like buying cattle." She made a motion as though swatting away a fly. "I'll talk to you all later about this."

Auctions, cattle, "getting" him—it all sounded rather Alice in Wonderlandish. And they even had a rabbit, albeit stuffed with sawdust.

"I'm Barden Granville, and I'll be responsible for dinner preparations here." He gave them what he hoped was a winning smile. "For the next six weeks at least."

Leonard scratched his cheek. "Where are you from, Bardy?"

He winced. His eldest brother, who would one day inherit Father's title, often teased him with that name. "I prefer to be called Barden or if you must Americanize it, please call me Bard."

"Bard? That's what they called Shakespeare, ain't it, Sis?" Leonard tapped the side of his head. "I'm soon to be graduated and some of Miss Green's teaching must have stuck."

"How about you all address me as Barden?" He checked with Mrs. Kane who gave him a noncommittal shrug.

Deanna rolled her eyes at her brother. "What town in England are you from, Barden? Are you from London?"

"Please, Deanna let the poor man get settled. Leonard go show him where the water pump is."

"Quite all right. I saw one."

"Good then." She opened the door to what was to be his room.

Dust covered almost every surface. "And I expect I shall require a great many trips up and down the stairs to put this room to rights."

From her shocked expression, he knew he'd been impertinent. If one of his servants had spoken to him in such a manner at home. . . "Please forgive my lack of manners."

"Since Pa died. . . I regret the deplorable condition of this room."

She was apologizing to him? To her new servant? Things certainly were different here in America.

Saturday night was their family meeting time, after the restaurant had closed for the evening. With the auditions over, the clean-up done, coping with all the guests, and introducing their new worker, the inn had been busy. Caroline and her siblings pushed the four middle tables together, grabbed their favorite chairs and arranged them. Henry and Leonard had theirs close together and slumped into them. Virginia and Deanna sat far apart and they began to arrange their skirts so they could sit.

Alvin still stood, solo, peering down at her. When had he gotten so tall? "You sure you trust that Englishman back there in the kitchen by himself?"

"Someone has to cover for us." Virginia shrugged. "With all these extra folks here."

Grimacing, Alvin slumped into his chair. "Luke's been helping out an awful lot. We ought to hire him on."

"I agree." Caroline sank onto her oak chair. "We have a lot more to discuss, too."

Deanna beamed. "Yes, like how Barden is handsomer than anyone around these parts."

"What about me?" Leonard feigned a slap, across the table.

The fifteen-year-old swatted at the air near him. "You're my brother."

Caroline cleared her throat. "Before we discuss Mr. Granville. . ."

"He said to call him Barden." Deanna squared her shoulders.

"Yeah." Leonard lifted his chin.

"Told me that, too." Eighteen-year-old Virginia examined her fingernails.

Alvin simply grunted.

Was it really worth arguing over?

"Besides, don't you mean we'll discuss your future husband?" Virginia drawled. When she batted her eyelashes, the others laughed—except Caroline.

Deanna pressed her hands rested her head on her hands and sighed. "Mrs. Barden Granville has a nice ring to it."

"A ring." Henry slapped the table. "Is that a pun?"

"A good one." Leonard clapped.

Giggles erupted from the girls.

"A big gold ring with an English crest on it, I bet." Virginia's face took on a dreamy expression.

The sound of dishes clattering in the kitchen quieted them all.

Alvin groaned. "Wonder how many more this Barden fellow just broke?"

"He hasn't broken anything." Not yet. And especially not Caroline's heart. "Anyway, let's discuss the letter first."

Deanna scowled. "Why did Lorraine have it anyway?"

Good point. Caroline shook her head as she opened the missive. She hesitated, something stirring in her soul. "First let's pray."

Although they all bowed their heads, she knew Henry would likely poke at Leonard and Alvin wouldn't keep his eyes closed. Deanna likely wouldn't listen to the prayer. But God knew all these things. "Heavenly Father, we ask your guidance as we discuss this letter from our. . ." Did she refer to them as grandparents? She'd never even met them. ". . .kin. May our hearts hear what You wish for us to know. Lord, guide us. We trust you and love you. In Jesus's name, Amen."

Alvin had one eye pressed closed and the other fixed on her. "Just who are these kin?"

A lump formed in her throat. How would she manage if they all wanted to go? She'd be alone. She'd have no help. And Pa had wanted her to do right by her brothers and sisters. Wouldn't letting them go, if they wished, be disregarding Pa's wishes? "Our grandparents in Virginia."

Deanna's brown eyebrows rose to her bangs. "In Virginia?"

"Yes."

They all looked at one another before fixing their gazes on her. Alvin assumed an air of nonchalance, leaning one arm around his chair back.

Leonard shoved a hand through his dark hair. "We don't know them."

"This would be one way to do that." Caroline hoped her tone of voice conveyed a conviction she lacked.

"Pa hated them." Virginia may have spoken the truth, but it sounded so harsh coming from her pretty sister.

Caroline cringed. She didn't want to sugarcoat things, but. . . "Pa didn't exactly hate them. They'd cut off relations with Ma after she married Pa."

"He very much didn't like them then." Virginia's lips curled into a pout, as though she was challenging Caroline to refute that.

"Pa didn't like what they did. It hurt Ma real bad."

How many times had Ma said she wished she could have contact with her family but she knew it would upset Pa? *Too many times to count.*

All at once, her sisters and brothers began chattering over top of one another and Caroline couldn't make out words other than the repetitive "Ma said" and "Pa said."

"Hush!"

"Do you want us to go?" Moisture pooled in her youngest sister's eyes.

"Of course not, Deanna. But some of you are getting to the age where you might want more than I. . . than life can give you here in Kansas."

Alvin muttered an oath.

"Alvin!"

"Sorry." The tone of his mumbled apology was anything but sorrowful.

"Let me read the letter to you. How about that?"

She surveyed the table as one by one they nodded in agreement. Alvin crossed his arms over his chest. The buttons strained. Not only was he getting taller but he was putting on more muscle. Soon he'd need to make decisions for himself about his future, regardless of where he lived.

Caroline opened up the letter and read. When she'd finished reading, all sat in stunned silence.

Henry rocked slightly in his chair. Leonard tapped his index finger on the gingham covered tabletop.

"They have a large home on the James River." A former plantation that they indicated was fairly intact because they'd been occupied by the Union Army.

Virginia squared her shoulders. "Of course I'm too old to go. But are they going to put Deanna and the boys to work in the fields? I've read in *Ladies Home Newsletter* that some Southern women are doing that."

"Oh my!" Deanna's cheeks flushed pink. "Will we have to pick cotton?"

More protests went up. "I don't believe so." But she didn't know these people at all.

"But I'm almost out of school." Leonard scowled. "If they want to do anything for me they can send me to medical training."

The kitchen door squeaked.

"I don't want to go." Henry slapped his hand down on the table, so much like Pa used to do that Caroline could only stare at the boy. Truth be told, her youngest brother was her favorite. She didn't want him away either.

Barden wheeled Ma's coffee service cart into the room. "What's a family gathering without some treats?"

"Yeah!" Henry clapped.

"Why don't we ask Barden his opinion?" Virginia fluttered her eyelashes as she peered up at him.

"Got somethin' in your eye?" Leonard reached across to poke at Virginia, and she swatted him away.

Mr. Granville cleared his throat. "Ask my opinion about what?"

As he expertly poured Caroline her evening tea, she looked up at him. This was a family matter. But what if he was to become her husband? "My maternal grandparents have come forward to request my brothers and sisters. . ."

Virginia arched an eyebrow. "Sister as in Deanna. I'm eighteen and have no need of grandparents to watch over me."

As he set the teacup down into its saucer, Barden leaned in close. "And what say you of this agenda?"

"She's again' it!" Henry affected a deep drawl and made a comical face. "Again' it, I say!"

The others laughed.

"I dare say, if you purport that she's against this dastardly plot, then why would you accept it?"

"I don't." Alvin rolled his eyes. "I'm enlisting in the army first chance I get."

"I'm not going anywhere." Virginia pointed at Caroline. "She's promised to send me to Normal School in Ohio to be a teacher."

"I did." Caroline muttered the words softly, although how she'd ever secure the funds she didn't know.

Barden pointed at the other three siblings in succession. "And how far away are said grandmama and grandpapa?"

"Over a thousand miles." Henry sank his head onto his hands. "I don't wanna go anyhow."

"Me neither." Deanna wrinkled her nose. "I'm almost grown. If I went anywhere, it would be up North. I've heard the soldiers are heading to a beautiful place."

Caroline cast her sister a wary look. Was Deanna getting notions, too?

Barden set a tray of golden cookies on the table. "Mrs. Freeman's sugar cookies."

As he continued to pour tea, Caroline watched in amazement as her brothers and sisters dug into the cookies. Had Frank been there, he'd have insisted each person take a turn and discuss the pros and cons of the decision to be made. Yet here, in under five minutes, Barden had convinced her brothers and sisters to see things her way.

Caroline blinked back tears. Having another husband might not be so bad after all.

Chapter Four

Early June, 1866

Who'd have thought the image of a man washing dishes could be so attractive? Caroline stood slicing potatoes at the work counter behind Barden, watching him. With a white linen towel casually draped over one shoulder, he hummed as he scoured dishes at the dry sink. Then he transferred those he'd washed to another tub and poured rinse water over them. His blue cotton shirt was tucked neatly into his work trousers and his leather belt shone from a recent polishing. Yesterday he'd brought in tightly woven cotton and linen toweling material purchased from the mercantile. Mr. Woodson had cut the rectangles and then Mae had sewn the towels on the treadle machine she had at her house. They did look nice. But why was Barden trying to change everything?

Mr. Woodson whistled off-key as he carried a load of wood to the pile beside the stove. "Your older sister must be mighty bored to be fraternizin' with us workers again."

"Why is Lorraine here anyway?" Caroline always marveled at the older man's way of getting straight to the point.

Barden turned to face the workman. "We're grateful for the relief she offers us—Mrs. Kane in particular."

Mr. Woodson gaped, and Caroline could only blink. But, it was true that Caroline had been allowed to sleep longer that day, because of her older sister's presence.

Noisy footsteps announced Lorraine's return to the kitchen. "There's a bunch of soldiers out there, Caroline."

"Soldiers?"

Virginia rushed in, her cheeks flushed, her ebony hair trailing ringlets around her ivory neck. She fanned herself with her hand, eyes wide. "A passel of handsome Army men are out there!"

"For the inn or the restaurant?" They had a business to run.

"They're on the move to Fort Mackinac." Lorraine squirreled a handkerchief from her apron pocket and dabbed at her forehead. "Which they've been writing about in the paper."

Caroline had never heard of this place. Was this what Deanna had been referring to as up North? "Where is that?"

Virginia batted at the air as if waving something away. "Far away from here."

Raising his index finger, Barden interjected, "I read about that fort in one of my Beadle's. We Brits took Fort Mackinac back from the Americans in the War of 1812."

Mr. Woodson scowled at him. "Better watch yerself, young fella, my Pa served in that war."

Again, her younger sister Virginia waved their comments away. "But there are a dozen soldiers out there and all but the commander are single."

Barden crossed his arms over his chest. "We've sent your application for the Ohio Normal School. And also letters asking for teaching posts that don't require additional training. Certainly, you don't entertain the notion that you'll be running off to a fort somewhere?"

Caroline gaped at the man. He'd taken the very words from her mouth, albeit spoken with a heavy British accent.

"Well they're here, and I've no position, do I?" Virginia scowled at them, her face settling back into its usual expression. But oh, what a delight to have seen her beautiful eighteen-year-old smile again even if for that moment.

Lorraine went to the stove and grabbed the coffee pot. "We'll need more coffee if they're anything like our ranch hands."

"As I've offered before, madam, I'm completely at your disposal if you ever need an extra pair of hands at the ranch."

Lorraine, Virginia, Mr. Woodson, and Caroline all stared at Barden as the room fell silent save for the sound of the stove and its contents bubbling.

Barden dried his hands and removed the heavy canvas apron. "Let me handle this."

First he'd offered to run off to her sister's. Now he behaved as if he was the man of this place. She should have objected. Caroline should have insisted it was her duty as owner to ascertain the needs of the military passing through. Instead, she sank onto the stool by the counter and stared at the pitiful pile of potatoes. If a dozen soldiers supped with them tonight, she'd need her efforts multiplied like the fishes and the loaves. Mercifully, funds from the auditions' rental had replenished their coffers. After school the previous day, Henry and Leonard had toted home flour, sugar, coffee, bacon and more from the mercantile.

Mae Reed entered through the back door, carrying with her the faint odor of liniment and spearmint. Her usual slow shuffle had improved to a steadier gait, with her back straighter too. "Good morning! How're you all doing this fine morning?"

"You sound well." Mr. Woodson smiled at Mae.

"Slept better than I have in a while, thanks to Barden's suggestion."

Caroline stiffened. Barden's list of "suggestions" for the inn and restaurant now topped fifty items. "And what was that?"

"He had me substitute chamomile tea for my evening coffee. That seemed to make a difference. Didn't wake up at all last night."

"Well, good. . ." What else could she say? It was wonderful news. If only his ever-lengthening list of ideas were good. Some were downright ridiculous. Number 20 was – *Make the evening meal one of charm and grace*. Number 21 - *Bring in more candles to supplement the lamps*. Number 22 - *Set out tablecloths*. Caroline had snorted over that idea. And who did he expect to launder all those table coverings?

Barden re-entered the kitchen, a soldier in federal blue uniform trailing him. *What in the world?* Caroline pushed aside her potatoes, stood, and smoothed her apron, all the while fixing a glare on Barden that she hoped would convey her dissatisfaction with his behavior. Guests didn't belong in the kitchen.

From the crimson blossoming on his cheeks, Barden evidently sensed her ire. The officer appeared nonplussed however. He held his hat tucked under his arm as he stepped forward and nodded curtly. "Captain John Mitchell, Company B, 43rd Regiment of Infantry, honored to make your acquaintance, ma'am."

She had no idea what that meant but nodded.

His gaze settled on Mae, who looked up at him in expectation. "How many men do you have, Captain?"

"Fifty-seven total."

Caroline felt her eyes widen.

"Only twelve are being allowed to stay in town, though."

Although they could use the extra income, she, her family, and the staff were plum worn out from the influx of men for the auction. She pressed a hand to her chest.

Barden lifted his chin and caught Caroline's eye. "The captain asked about baths for his men, and I believe we have a way to accommodate them."

"Those here will have fresh water, soap and clean towels in their rooms." Caroline shrugged.

The Captain cleared his throat. "Mr. Granville thought all of my men might bathe."

The kitchen seemed to be getting as hot as her temper. "We have only one tub here at the inn."

Barden grinned. "Well, the saloon could be used, if the sheriff would allow us access."

Not a bad idea if it wasn't one of so many brilliant notions the Englishman had. The tavern had at least two man-sized steel tubs in the back room and a stove as large as the inn's.

"I think you'd best ask our mayor, Abigail Melton, first."

Barden's smile wobbled. "I purchased the extra wood, already."

"Oh?" Another action he'd not discussed with her. He was beginning to remind her more of Frank and of the things he'd done that had irked her. Things she'd not thought of in the past two years.

"I was certain you wouldn't mind. It was after all needed and an act of Christian charity."

She wasn't running a charity but a business, but they'd have to have a discussion later.

Lorraine not so subtly eyed the Captain. "The barber could help. He has a good-sized tub."

"Wonderful notion." The commander stroked his moustache which looked in need of grooming.

Who'd heard of army men wanting a soak and scrub? "Don't your soldiers simply bathe in the river, Captain Mitchell?"

"Not all are able, ma'am. You see, while I have an infantry unit, most of my men are wounded, some severely."

"Oh." Caroline sank back onto the stool. "Injured, yet they are traveling to another fort?"

The man's ruddy complexion became redder still. "Yes, you see many wish to serve out their commission. The Michigan fort is a light duty fort where my men can recover from the war."

Embarrassed at having questioned the officer, Caroline's lips parted to apologize, but she couldn't manage what to say. She exchanged a glance with Barden. No wonder he'd immediately sought to do something to help the men. One thing she'd learned about him, right away, was his compassion for others. It was touching.

Barden winked at her and then waved toward her, Mae, and Mr. Woodson. "Captain Mitchell, I know I speak for all when I say we are quite happy to meet the needs of your men. Furthermore, tomorrow night you and your officers staying at the inn will be our first guests to experience our new evening dining menu. Suffice it to say, it shall be more suitable for the officers than what we normally offer. And we hope soon to provide this service to all our guests."

Caroline fixed a smile on her face. Had the cat gotten her tongue, wound it up like a ball of yarn, and then unrolled it to the next county over? Just when she'd been admiring his compassionate nature, Barden Granville dumps this surprise on her?

This would have to be nipped in the bud!

Barden opened the back door of the restaurant for Mae then turned and called over his shoulder, "We'll be right back, Luke." As he escorted the widow to her home, he hummed an American Stephen Foster song one of the soldiers had earlier played on his banjo.

"That was one of my husband's favorite tunes, bless his soul." She carefully took the three wide steps up onto her porch.

The two-story brick home featured a wraparound porch. Large, mullioned windows fronted the house on either side, with a wide paneled center door. Maybe Barden had gotten ahead of himself in suggesting they improve the evening meals both in substance and appearance. In future, when he settled in his new church, would he be forced to ask matrons to share their household goods if there was a parish-wide event?

"Are you sure you feel comfortable with this, Mrs. Reed?"

"Of course, dear. My china and silver are sitting unused." She patted the side of her hair, twisted up and held in place with a large tortoise comb. "Using fine things makes a meal more special, don't you think?"

"I do." He rubbed his chin. "I thought my conversation went rather well with Mrs. Kane earlier, don't you?" He'd laid out all the reasons why the Tumble Inn might wish to spruce up not only its appearance but try to attract a more refined crowd.

Only the sound of a key turning in the lock met his ears, much like Mrs. Kane's silence earlier. Mrs. Reed tucked the large key back into her apron pocket and pushed open the door. Inside, the cozy parlor, on the left, looked like the place a cowboy would love to come home to. A sturdy velvet-covered chaise rested before a wall of books ensconced in a splendid walnut case. An overstuffed armchair was matched by a stool upon which a man might rest his feet after a long day rounding up cattle. A tea table held a silver tea service.

He could picture his wife bringing in afternoon tea for him after a hard day on the trail. Why did that image suddenly include a lovely young woman whose auburn hair begged him to bury his face in it every time she drew too near? He could picture a roaring fire glowing in the fireplace on a chill autumn night. Peyton Shiloh, the hero of one of his favorite dime novels, would surely applaud this parlor as perfect. It wouldn't be, though, without the American woman who'd begun to give him more reason to love America than any of his books had.

"Are you all right, Barden?" Mae crossed the hallway to another front-facing room. Barden followed her.

An oval cherrywood table was flanked at each end by shell-backed armchairs. Two matching armless chairs faced another pair across the table. Such furniture would only be found in a wealthy rancher's home. "What did you say your husband did?"

"He was a surgeon." She wiped something from her eyes and turned her back to him as she faced a glass-fronted hutch, filled with plates, bowls, and saucers.

She began to remove some of the plates, but the deformity in her hands caused her to struggle.

"Let me help."

Soon they had three sets of complete china place settings. "I had my mother's china, mine, and my grandmother's. I was the only daughter. When we came to Kansas, we had this all packed and shipped. Nary a piece was broken."

Although not nearly as fine as those at the Cheatham Hall estate, the three patterns were of high quality. "They're lovely. Are you certain you wish to engage in this dining experiment with me at the inn?"

"I would flat out love to see these dishes get some use. Life is short, Barden. No use storing up our treasures here on earth. Like the good Book says."

"Indeed." What earthly goods he had brought with him to America had been taken from him. But God had provided in most unusual ways.

"And I should tell you Caroline is a creature of habit. Not much for change. But she needs to do so if that inn is going to make it."

He had only a short time he could help. And Caroline hadn't yet mentioned when he'd be paid for his duties. "We'll get her off to a good start."

The petite woman's eyebrows wove together. "What do you mean *to a good start*?"

Perhaps it was wisest not to disclose when he must return to tend his flock. And he still wished to fulfill his goal. "Well, you see I really wished to experience the cowboy life before I settle down."

"Ah. . ." Her lower lip drooped. "So you would hop on a chance to work at a ranch if you had the opportunity?"

"I'm afraid so. As you said, life is short. This has been a lifelong dream of mine." He offered her what he hoped was a charming smile.

"Well, I'm sure Mrs. Martinchek would be happy to have you provide relief help if you must fulfill your cowboy yearnings before. . ."

"Hello!" Caroline's older sister entered the house. "I could have sworn I heard my name just now."

"You did, dear. It seems Barden wishes to try cowboy life before settling down."

"Yes, before I assume my vocation, I wish to learn more about ranching."

Both women eyed him.

A smirk twitched at Mrs. Martinchek's lips. "Vocation? I've never heard it put that way."

He prayed they didn't question what his vocation was. That had been a deal between himself and God when he'd come on this journey. Not that the Lord made deals, but Barden had offered one. He'd not share he was a vicar, and when he returned to England, he'd be the best parish priest he could be.

Oh but how he'd been tempted to tell Caroline. *Lord, guide me.*

Chapter Five

Caroline crumpled Barden's note about the painting crew he'd hired and the cost incurred and then stuffed it into her pocket. Standing outside the inn, and peering up, she'd have to agree. Yes, the paint was peeling. Yes, it needed to be done. But it seemed as soon as the Englishman tackled one idea, he'd moved on to the next.

Lord, this cannot be the kind of man you'd put me with. Leastwise on a permanent basis.

The new sheriff, a handsome man, rode by and tipped his hat at her. She offered him a tight smile. Abigail and he made a mighty fine-looking couple, even if those two were like she and Barden were—oil and water.

She wadded the note, in her pocket, into a tiny ball. If the auditions were ridiculous then his fancying up the dinner was even more so. To allow their new cook, and her future husband, to sweep in and begin changing up things would have been something Pa would have put a stop to. But Pa wasn't here. Her husband Frank wasn't someone who had grand ideas. His one big idea had been serving in the Civil War. And he'd died before he could enlist. Poor Frank. But at least he'd been spared that horror.

Opening the front door to the restaurant, she searched for Barden. He wasn't in the dining room, which had been swept, mopped, windows cleaned, walls scrubbed, and new tablecloths laid down. But no meal had been started yet and Mae was lying down, so she didn't wish to disturb her. Caroline wove through the kitchen. The back counter was covered with the new dish towels, presumably over top the rolls they'd be eating that night.

"Barden's outside."

She exited the building. She needed to know what to have the boys and Deanna do when they arrived home from school.

She found Barden sitting at her mother's bench, head bent as though he was in deep thought. "What all do you have for tonight?"

"Oh! Yes. Looks like several of the soldiers are amputees, a few with sword wounds, two with minie balls still inside them. . ."

"No! I meant the meal." For someone whose primary purpose was to feed customers, Barden seemed awfully preoccupied with their life situation. "What are you serving them?"

"Oh." Barden grinned, sending a warmth through her. He stood and took her hand and her heart began beating harder. "I'd rather keep it a surprise."

She despised surprises. All of the surprises she'd had in her life had been horrid, up until now. She pulled her hand free. "Seriously. What are you feeding those soldiers?"

Cocking his head at her, Barden eyed her carefully. "You don't trust me to make a good decision, do you?"

Caroline placed her hands on her hips, the plaid material bunching there in a wave of turquoises and blues. "You're making many changes and decisions."

Barden laughed. "Well, then, I'm making one now. Go up and rest milady, before your feast is served this evening."

Henry and Leonard carried a crate, each holding a loop of rope that extruded from each side.

Her soon-to-be-husband turned and held out his hand. "Stop right there, gentlemen. We don't want to have Caroline guessing my menu, now do we?"

A small cart pulled by a brown and white pony stopped in the alleyway. Deanna called out, "Come on, Caroline, I'm taking you for a ride!"

Barden gestured for her to go on. "Don't fret."

Why on earth she was caving in so easily to this Englishman's demands, Caroline couldn't articulate. But she soon found herself in the cart with her dark-haired sister whisking her away.

"I'm to get you a new hair bow and I'm purchasing ribbons for myself and I would for Virginia, too, if she wasn't being such a fussbudget this morning."

"What do you mean?"

"She was ornery toward me. Said I was a little girl and she was a young woman and that she no longer wore ribbons in her hair nor did she wish for Barden to buy her anything."

"Barden?"

"Yes. He gave me some money to get us something." Deanna clucked her tongue at the pony to urge her on. "He was so sweet. Said he wished he could purchase us all a whole new wardrobe, but he couldn't."

A whole new wardrobe. Wouldn't that be something? Why would such a notion even cross his mind? Perhaps because he knew he brought nothing to the marriage. Caroline drew in a slow breath. She really should ask him more about himself. He'd said he'd grown up in England and had older brothers. His father did something for the government and his mother stayed at home, presumably taking care of the family. What kind of parents allowed their educated son to run off to America, though? Truth be told, with knowing Frank all his life, it hadn't been until they'd married that she really understood him better. And it would likely be the same with Barden. He'd tell her more when he was good and ready—like most men.

Three hours later, dressed in her best apricot-colored sateen church dress, Caroline descended the stairs. Her hands brushed over the freshly waxed banisters, the scent of lemon oil still lingering in the air. Pa wouldn't have wanted Caroline to have continued in what he called her "widow's weeds," and it was time to give them up, regardless of convention.

Her sister Virginia's eyes glowed tonight. For the first time since her sweetheart had died, a year earlier, she'd changed out of solid dark clothing and into a floral-patterned dress of icy yellow, soft pinks and cream. She led Caroline to a white cloth covered table. Although most of the candle holders in the restaurant didn't match, the glowing candles did add a festive light to the lamps that hung from holders on the walls.

Captain Mitchell stood, bowed from the waist and pulled Caroline's chair from the table. The other two men attempted to rise. Lieutenant Andrews, she'd been told earlier, was missing one leg. The other man was weak from ongoing sickness from the injuries he'd received in the war.

"Please, gentlemen, remain seated."

Both nodded as Mitchell helped her. Caroline accommodated for the stiff crinoline beneath her skirt as she settled into the chair.

"A great idea, ma'am, of fancyin' things up for the men." Andrews removed the cloth napkin from the table and spread it across his lap.

"It'll lift their spirits." The captain scanned the room, which was filled with men all attired in their uniforms, all clean and neat.

Caroline laughed. "I think it is already cheering me up, too."

Barden strode through the entrance from the kitchen, dressed in a close-fitting suit that she recognized as being one of Dr. Reed's. The dark wool jacket and matching trousers made him appear taller, and if possible even more handsome. He carried a massive silver platter covered with roast beef slices. Displaying it in that fashion made it appear much more appealing. The beef ranged from a reddish rare to a fully browned well done.

Steam rose from the platter as he approached their table. "Madam, choose your slice."

Caroline pointed out a piece with just a hint of pink. "How on earth did you manage this?"

Captain Mitchell tapped the side of his temple. "Let's just say that the mayor is a charming woman and that the tavern now smells strongly of roast beef."

"That explains it. No wonder there'd been no scent of meat cooking."

The captain grinned.

Her sisters brought gravy boats into the room while Henry and Leonard served rolls with crocks of fresh butter. Alvin carried around bowls of whipped potatoes.

"We're trying to offer our guests a lovely dinner but with a family feel." Barden smiled down at her.

What would life with this man be like? Would he always be coming up with ideas?

Virginia lingered near one table in particular, and Alvin at another. Her sister stared in rapt attention at a handsome private with dark wavy hair and a moustache. He resembled the sweetheart her poor sister had lost in the war. Caroline averted her gaze. So many of their town men gone, never to return.

"I understand your brother wishes to enlist, Mrs. Kane." Captain Mitchell paused in slicing his almost-red rare piece of beef.

Caroline stifled the urge to gag. Somehow the image of the almost raw meat, a military captain, and the mention of her brother's name as a possible soldier contrived to make her feel ill. "Alvin is quite young and he's of much help to us here."

Lieutenant Andrews swallowed the half roll he'd shoved into his mouth. "I reckon he's older'n I was when I enlisted."

"Older than David, too." Captain Mitchell gestured with Mrs. Reed's silver fork toward a smooth-faced boy huddled at the far end of a table, focused only on eating his food. "He's sixteen."

"Sixteen?" Caroline stiffened.

"He'll learn a lot at a fort like Mackinac – with all these seasoned veterans there."

She glanced at the corner table, where Luke Collins was conversing with his fiancé. If there was another war, would young David suffer what her newest employee had? "What of his parents? His family?"

Andrews and Mitchell exchanged a brief glance before both shook their heads.

Best not pursue that topic. Caroline shifted the conversation to the weather and travel, and soon they were discussing the difficulties of a cross-country trip. Alvin and

Virginia continued to linger at their respective stops as the soldiers passed the potatoes themselves and poured their gravy.

When Barden strolled through the room, Caroline tugged at his elbow. As he bent near, she inhaled his spicy sandalwood scent. A little light-headed, she managed to get out her request. "Can you please check on Virginia and Alvin? They're spending excessive time at those tables."

He nodded, then straightened. After circling the room, he discreetly stopped to talk with each sibling, who then moved on back to the kitchen.

"Have you ever been to Michigan, Mrs. Kane?" Captain Mitchell grabbed another roll and dipped it into his gravy.

"I've never lived outside of Kansas." Other than in her fantasies, where she lived in late 18th century England surrounded by servants and in love with a man who was the epitome of gentlemanly courtliness. *No wonder poor Frank Kane couldn't live up to my expectations.*

"I hear it is a beautiful place where the fort is situated, but winters can be brutal."

"The lakes are as large as seas." Andrews lifted his chin, a dab of potatoes dotting his cheek. She resisted the urge to wipe it for him and touched her own face in the same spot hoping he'd take the hint. He didn't.

"But the straits around the island freeze in the winter—it's that cold!" Captain Mitchell feigned shivering.

"So you can walk to the mainland." The lieutenant, finally sensing something, wiped his face with his hand.

Mitchell frowned. "If you dare."

What did she dare do? Barden strode toward them, his eyes fixed on her, his smile doing something that launched butterflies in her stomach.

He touched her shoulder and leaned in. "Are you ready for coffee to be served?"

"Or tea?" She resisted the urge to cover his hand with hers. How could such a simple touch set her heart racing?

He grinned, a dimple appearing in one cheek.

"A shame there's no spirits served." Captain Mitchell scanned the room. Was he looking for a liquor cabinet? "The men prefer their beer or liquor."

"Shame there's none to be had." Andrews patted his chest, as though feeling for a bottle.

Caroline straightened in her chair. "Coffee or tea will go well with our dessert." Not that she knew what Mae and Barden had come up with but there had been a tremendous amount of whipping cream, crumbling of stale cake, and a pan of pudding prepared plus jars of jelly opened.

"It's a trifle." Barden beamed in apparent self-satisfaction.

Kitchen work wasn't trifling. It was hard. Bone wearying hard. "I beg to differ, as I viewed the results of that dessert preparation."

Captain Mitchell laughed. "I believe Mr. Granville means it's called trifle—a kind of English cake and custard concoction."

"Oh. What an unusual name for a dessert. Especially when the mess in the kitchen from preparing it was no trifling matter."

The men laughed, but she'd not meant to be funny. Caroline's cheeks heated. Barden withdrew his hand from her shoulder.

Mr. Woodson emerged from the kitchen, a huge glass punch bowl in his arms. From across the room she spied the pretty layers of white for the cake, red for the jelly, pale yellow for the custard pudding, all topped by a cloud of whipped cream.

The men clapped and a few whistled, making Caroline's ears ring. Someone suddenly strummed on a banjo.

Barden leaned back in, his face so close to hers she could kiss him if she swiveled toward him. "Do you approve?" His murmur stirred a longing in her.

Did she approve of kissing in public? No, he couldn't read her mind. He meant the trifle. Caroline turned toward him, grasped the back of his neck, and pulled his face closer, choosing at the last minute to plant a kiss on his cheek.

"Thank you, Barden."

Hoots ensued. But the raucous laughter didn't surprise her as much as did Barden's reaction. For his face turned several shades paler as he hastily departed the room.

Oh heavens, no. Barden had seen that look before in the eyes of a young lady in one of the parish flocks he'd visited as a priest in training. When he'd gone to put his vestments away, in a back room of the country church, the girl had popped out like a jack-in-the-box and grabbed him and kissed him before he could stop her. If the parish priest hadn't been only steps behind him, Barden could have been in a world of trouble. As it was, he returned to school and had been warned of the strange proclivity some young ladies had toward men of the cloth. But he wasn't in England. And he wasn't a vicar. *Not yet.*

Barden pressed his fingertips to where Caroline had kissed his cheek, leaving him wanting more yet knowing he'd be leaving soon. He had to lay his cards on the table, figuratively speaking. Although look where that had literally gotten him last time he'd done so. Thank God for the Freemans, who'd sheltered him.

Leonard, Henry, and Mae had cleaned up almost all of the pots and pans and bowls and were starting on the soup bowls.

The kitchen door swung in and Caroline joined them, frowning. But when she looked beyond him, at the orderly kitchen, she beamed. "You all have done so well at getting things washed and cleaned."

Leonard tapped the pot he was drying. "Barden promised us a ride out to Lori's ranch if we did a bang-up job."

Barden drew closer to the youth and tapped his shoulder. "Which you did."

"You promised what?" His employer's voice held a warning.

"Mrs. Martinchek said I was welcome to come out on my day off. . ."

"Day off? I don't get a day off." Caroline's scoff almost sounded like she was holding back tears.

His eyebrows tugged together. She was the owner and could choose whether she'd take a day to herself. "But I do receive time off, like the others. Do I not?"

Her mouth agape, Caroline cocked her head at him, reminding him of a beautiful canary from the hotel where he'd stayed in New York, upon arrival. "I suppose you do."

Now didn't seem like the time to ask about his wages. He clapped his hands. "There. Righto. It's settled then."

Her eyes took on a misty sheen. "I wish you'd ask me first."

He'd never been much on asking. Barden simply did and often paid for the consequences later. Not a very priestly trait, but it was how God had made him. Or perhaps his privileged upbringing had brought this about. "I. . . could start doing that." It might kill him, but he could try. Especially since he'd be answering to a board and to his superiors come autumn.

"I'll go with you all." Caroline's lips formed a perfect pout. "It's time I had a day off, too."

Mr. Woodson carried the empty trifle bowl into the kitchen. "Ya'll goin' somewhere?"

Mae took it and set it into the dishpan. "They're going out to the ranch tomorrow."

The handyman turned toward Caroline. "I'll hold down the fort, ma'am. No trouble at all as long as Mae helps me."

"Sure thing." Mae beamed at Woodson and then winked at Barden. "If I were younger I'd want to come out there myself and watch our very own Englishman on the ranch."

Their own? How would she and the others feel when he departed? Yet he, too, had begun to think of these people as "his own." He'd felt more a part of these Turtle Creek residents than he had in all his life at Cheatham Hall. It was as though he'd finally gotten where he was supposed to be.

Home.

Chapter Six

Muffled voices from the hallway woke Barden. Alvin and Virginia's tones were an odd rush of excitement mixed with anger.

"Let's ask Barden if he'll put in a word for us." Virginia's voice was clearer now, as though she stood immediately outside his room.

The sharp rap on the door was clearly Alvin's, which was confirmed when he slipped into the room holding a lamp, then closed the door behind him. "Sorry to disturb you."

"What is it?" Barden shifted up onto his elbows as the iron framed bed groaned in protest. "Anything wrong?"

In the lamplight, a dozen emotions flickered over the young man's angular face. "No."

"So you're accustomed to entering bedchambers uninvited?"

"No." Alvin ran his tongue over his lower lip. "I just wanted to ask before you and Caroline leave for the ranch."

"Which isn't for another hour or two."

"Yes, well. . ." Alvin shifted his weight side to side, reminding Barden of a pupil about to be disciplined by the headmaster.

"Out with it then."

"Virginia and I, we could use a day off, too, maybe even a couple of days to go visit some of the places that have teacher openings."

What a thoughtful brother. Although he hated to admit it, Barden would not have thought Alvin harbored much interest in anyone beside himself, which was entirely normal for a boy that age. "Commendable."

A strange smile tugged at Alvin's lips. "Someone has to look after her."

"Right you are. I'll put in a good word for you."

This time only unfettered glee lit Alvin's face. How long had it been since any of the Tumblestons had left Turtle Springs for an outing? "Thanks."

"At your service." Barden made a whisking motion with his hand. "Now be off so I can get ready."

After Alvin left, Barden quickly dressed, stopped in at the kitchen for breakfast, tossed scraps to the two stray dogs in the alley, and washed. Then he grabbed the coffee pot and carried it into the restaurant.

Barden caught Virginia's eye. Hard to believe such a lovely young lady had already lost her beau. Back in England, they had heard about America's warring upon itself, but he'd never imaged the toll in human lives it had taken. *Truly shocking.* Perhaps that was why she had such a great interest in the young soldier she stood near. "Why don't you sit for a moment, Miss Tumbleston, while I pour for our guests?"

The private jumped to his feet and pulled out a chair beside him. Virginia blushed but sat, arranging her skirts around her.

Alvin lingered by Captain Mitchell and his officers, seated at the center table, plates piled high with food.

Caroline's brother spoke with more animation than Barden had observed during the weeks prior, his broad hands punctuating his words. The officers nodded.

When Barden approached the table, they became silent. "Good day, gentlemen."

"Mornin', pardner." Andrews chuckled. "Hear you're going to be a ranch hand today."

"I reckon I'll try." Barden's attempt at a cowboy accent was dreadful.

Alvin rolled his eyes. "And I reckon I'll get back to the kitchen."

Andrews tapped his index finger on the oilcloth covered table. "We'll speak with you later, young man."

Alvin ducked his chin and headed off, his step jaunty as he went.

"Maybe we can help you out, too." Lieutenant Andrews held up his mug for a refill of coffee.

How were they helping Alvin? It wasn't his place to ask. "Oh how so?"

"We're not cowboys." Captain Mitchell chuckled. "But our sharp shooters can give you some training on fire arms."

Barden stifled a laugh. "Very kind of you. But unnecessary."

"No, no, we insist." Lieutenant Andrews shoved an entire biscuit into his mouth.

Captain Mitchell tugged on his now neatly trimmed moustache. "You've treated us so well."

"Here's a tip—try to keep your behind in the saddle, too, when you're riding." Andrews laughed, sending biscuit crumbs onto the napkin covering his blue uniform.

"We'd like to help you with at least one cowboy skill." Mitchell was obviously used to having his commands obeyed.

"No use wasting your time." Barden glanced around, making sure no one was within ear shot, and bent in to whisper. "I'm a crack shot."

From their wild guffaws, they mustn't believe him. He waited a moment.

"Good one!" Mitchell offered his cup to Barden for a refill. "An Englishman who cooks and obviously is accustomed to being a servant. We'll be over in the green, if you'd like some target practice before you go."

Hands shaking, Barden finished pouring coffee and then left the room, wishing he could punch something.

In the kitchen, Caroline packed a small basket with jars of lemonade and ham biscuits. "Mr. Woodson is bringing the wagon around. Do you mind heading out early?"

He set the pot where it could be refilled and rubbed his forehead.

"Are you all right, Barden?"

"I don't know. But I am well, if that is what you mean."

Her features tugged, as though she was working something out that perplexed her.

"Are all employers so thoughtful as you are, Mrs. Kane?"

Her mouth gaped open but then she closed it again. "You're right. We did have an agreement. Six weeks."

What that had to do with cordiality, he didn't know. As those six weeks began to draw to an end, though, he couldn't imagine how hard it would be to tell her he was returning to England. But without a paycheck from her yet and no word from Father's rancher friends, might he not be extending his stay? Unless he humbled himself and asked his father for the fare. "Well, I thank you for your thoughtfulness."

Before long, they were on their way to the ranch. He drove the rig, with Caroline nestled beside him. She remained quiet until they were just outside of town. Overhead, thick clouds gathered, and their dove gray underbellies cautioned him that they might have rain.

"Did you live in the countryside in England?" Caroline bunched a lace-trimmed handkerchief in her lap.

"Yes, I did. There were vast swaths of fields and forests and farmland."

"Sounds lovely."

Not as lovely as she was.

"Why did you leave? Did something bad happen?"

"Oh no, certainly not." But if he left America, something bad would happen to him—he'd be leaving Caroline behind.

"When you were living there, did you ever imagine what it would be like to be a mail-order groom?"

Barden began to laugh. What a notion! "Never!" Not that those men who'd just auditioned and found wives were to be mocked. He bit his tongue.

He took his eyes from the road to glance at her. Her face pinked up, making Caroline look even prettier, her lips inviting him to take his eyes fully from the road and kiss her. With that little copse of maple trees ahead, he could pull over to the side of the road, take her in his arms and. . .

"Barden?"

"Hmm?"

"But you did imagine that you would one day be married, didn't you?"

"Oh yes, of course." And to one of the feisty heroines in a Beadle's novel. An American woman. At least he was finally admitting the truth of his fantasies. He'd mulled over the notion that he would marry whatever proper Englishwoman who'd accept life with the third son of a nobleman. He and his wife might on occasion be invited to visit Cheatham Hall. Some ladies might be satisfied with such an arrangement. And there was the one professor's daughter who'd told him plainly that if his brothers both died and produced no heirs, then Barden would inherit and she'd be interested in being courted. His face flushed at the recollection. How a properly brought up young woman, the daughter of a religion professor, could make so light of his brothers' lives had repulsed him. He'd never spoken with her again.

Caroline sighed. "Marriage wasn't quite like I thought it would be."

He slowed the pair of bays as they crossed a deep rut. Caroline clutched the side of the seat.

As they emerged from the depression in the road, she sighed. "I'd known Frank all my life but I didn't really know him; if that makes any sense."

With regret, Barden contemplated his valet, Sinclair, who'd asked to come with him to America. Barden had been so taken aback. Perhaps he should have expected that from the man, whom he'd known all his life. Sinclair had fed his interest in American fiction, albeit of a questionable quality, and of Americans in general. "I know I let someone down, who I'd known since I was a child. I truly hadn't known his wishes. And I wasn't in a position to fulfill them." Perhaps if he'd been more thoughtful, more considerate of other's needs, then perchance he'd have realized and could have better planned.

"Frank didn't get the chance to fulfill any of his wishes. He wanted to go off and fight in the war, but he died of a terrible fever before he could enlist."

"But he had married you. That wish was met. God gave him that."

Soft sobs were accompanied by sniffs. He wanted to pull over and wrap his arms around her and comfort Caroline.

"God. . . has taken my mother, my husband. . ." she hiccupped. "Then He took Pa."

Barden exhaled a big puff of air. "I don't know why that happened, Caroline. But I do know that regardless, He loves you. He loved them."

"Doesn't. . .feel like it."

Barden passed the reins into one hand and pulled his handkerchief out from his vest pocket and pressed it into her hands. "I believe God knows all things. He loves us all. We are in a war with darkness. God knows the devil's plans. He'll take us to the heavenly realms when our life on earth no longer is the place for us to be. We're here but an infinitesimal time, compared to His eternity. We have to trust that God knows why and when we must join Him in glory."

Caroline sniffed, then gently blew her nose. "My father used to read us a passage that talked about God sparing us further difficulties that we couldn't bear up under."

"Yes, I believe that's in Isaiah."

Drawing in a shuddering breath, Caroline met his eyes. "I guess I just thought once Mama died, that I'd already done without enough."

Throwing all caution aside, Barden wrapped an arm around her and pulled her closer, kissing the top of her head. "I'm sorry you've gone through this, Caroline. I truly am. And I pray that the Lord will bless the rest of your life in abundance."

He was surprised when she didn't resist, but leaned toward him, as though this was the most natural thing in the world.

And it surely felt like it was. He could hold her like this forever, drawing in the sweet scent of lemon soap mixed with vanilla and sugar. Barden couldn't help smiling. This rush of emotions, of wanting to protect her yet at the same time wanting to kiss her silly had his senses roiling. Could he bring her back with him to the parish? Was there some way they could be together?

Pulling away from him, and looking up with wide eyes, Caroline exhaled a loud breath. "I think we best continue on."

"At your service." Barden kept Caroline close by his side, not wanting to release her, until he needed the use of both hands to steer the horses toward the turn to the Martinchek ranch.

When they got there, Joel jogged out from the barn to greet them. He assisted Caroline down and she rewarded her brother-in-law with a peck on his cheek.

Martinchek waved for one of the men to move the wagon. "Water the horses, too, while you're at it."

"Yes sir!" The blond man saluted his boss and then turned and winked at the rancher's wife, who had joined Caroline.

When Mrs. Martinchek scowled at the ranch hand, Barden felt a check in his spirit.

Caroline muttered under her breath, "Scotty better watch himself."

So she sensed it, too.

Barden jumped down onto the hard-packed earth and handed off the reins to the cocky cowboy, who wasn't quite as tall as him, but with a thick neck and muscles bulging his plaid cotton shirt.

Barden, wearing his only clean pair of trousers, a vest, and a broadcloth shirt probably didn't look as out of place on the ranch as he felt. But standing next to this ranch hand, he felt the fraud he was. Had he arrived in his clerical attire or even in his casual clothing from home, he'd have appeared as foreign as he felt. *But would I not, then, have been genuine?*

Scotty directed the horses to pull the wagon off to the side of the barn.

Beyond him, in fenced pastures that extended for acres, cattle munched on grass. In the barn loft, a ranch hand forked hay down below while others, outside, hauled buckets full of water to the troughs.

Barden inhaled the fresh scent of the hay, longing to run and join them. This was the sole reason for his jaunt across the ocean. But at every turn he'd been frustrated. *Why Lord?* And what had happened with Caroline back there? Something between them had shifted, had deepened into a friendship he didn't want to abandon. But he'd spent a lifetime awaiting this chance.

If he couldn't find cowboy experience in Turtle Creek, perhaps his godfather or his father's friends, who ranched in a small cow town many hours south, would finally reply to his telegram. Perhaps before he left he'd visit there, despite his father's wrath which would surely be invoked if he ever heard of Barden's doings.

Several massive dogs burst from the barn and headed straight at the wagon. Joel whistled but the dogs ignored their master. Barden stepped between Caroline and the animals as he assessed the situation. The oncoming dogs ranged from a yipping beagle to a wolfhound who might weigh more than Barden did.

"Jojo, stop!" Still the rancher's command had no effect.

When Barden perceived all three wagging their tails, he rummaged in his vest pocket for one of the treats he offered the stray dogs back at the inn. All three stopped and sat at his feet, reminding him so much of a hound pack after a hunt. After rubbing each of their heads, Barden divvied up the hard biscuit amongst the trio.

"Well played, old chap." Martinchek's attempt at a British accent was almost as dreadful as Barden's fake drawl. "I hear you've adopted several of Turtle Creek's strays."

"Even the least of God's creatures deserves some care."

"As one of the church deacons, I'd agree." The rancher jerked his thumb toward the hands, several sitting atop a fence rail. "Just don't be speaking too much of that around them. I don't like them thinking about what happens to all those cattle we drive to auction."

"I understand. And, Deacon Martinchek, I'm continuing to pray for the pastor." Especially since the inn's gossip was circulating that Reverend Smith might be retiring after he'd suffered his recent injury. At home, they'd send a supply minister if the vicar was ill or must travel. But apparently not in this part of America.

Joel looped his thumbs into his waistband. "The boys have been wanting to have a little fun. Do a shooting match. Are you up to it?"

Between the army officers and now this rancher, men were pushing for him to prove his mettle with a gun. Granted, such a skill was necessary with the number of rustlers around.

"I'd welcome the opportunity." If given the proper equipment.

"Well then, let's get our crew out here."

Caroline and Lorraine stood behind the row of men. "I can't believe Joel would allow Barden to humiliate himself like this."

"He wouldn't." Her sister patted the side of her flaxen hair, upswept with a dozen ringlets dangling from her neck.

"What do you mean?"

"I trust my husband. He's not that kind of man. I think he knows exactly what he's doing."

Had her sister gone plum loco over her husband? Lorraine certainly wanted only to be alone with Joel. She'd had Caroline and their siblings out to the ranch only a handful of times since the wedding. From the corner of her eye, Caroline watched Lorraine surreptitiously pull at the waistband of her Robin's egg blue skirt.

"Joel is the best rancher in these parts." Too bad he couldn't see what a dolt that Scotty was.

"Do you even know what Barden did before he came to Turtle Creek?"

"He worked at Mary and Uziah's place for a while."

"Mary sent me a letter. Someone has been looking for Barden. A big man. English, and older, but she wrote that he had meaty fists like a boxer."

"Oh my." Uziah Freeman had boxed for a while to earn his living before they'd bought the restaurant.

"You still have Pa's rifle in the kitchen don't you?"

Caroline's heartbeat hammered in her chest as the men loaded their guns.

Lorraine removed a small pistol from her skirt pocket and handed it to Caroline. "Some of the men who've come to town have turned out to be criminals."

"Not Barden. If anything, he sounds more like a. . ."

"A what?" Lorraine's lips turned downward in irritation.

"A preacher."

"A fine looking man like that?" Her sister laughed. "I think not."

Joel took aim at a line of cans and began to fire. Caroline flinched as her brother-in-law shot repeatedly, knocking over three of the seven cans.

"Gotta do better'n that, boss!" Scotty ambled across the yard and set up more cans.

When he returned, he shoved his broad hand through hair that matched Lorraine's color, and he winked up at her. "Watch this ladies!"

Didn't Joel even care how the man acted toward his wife?

Five of the seven went down.

When Scotty laughed and began to jog toward the hay bales, Barden called out. "I say, old chap, have you got something smaller?"

Lorraine frowned. "Smaller?"

Barden glanced in her direction. "Some small potatoes perhaps?"

"What?" Caroline cocked her head.

Within minutes, Lorraine had retrieved little potatoes from the root cellar and Scotty had set them up, mocking Barden as he placed them on the haystacks.

Both Caroline and Lorraine sat on the edge of the wooden bench as Barden began to fire. He hit every tiny potato.

Joel hooted. "Maybe our mayor should have hired you for sheriff."

"Sheriff Ingram got here first," Lorraine called out.

She turned to Caroline. "You better find out more about him and what he's up to."

Yes, she did.

"I think you'd make a right fine cowboy and if Caroline ever cuts you loose from the Tumble Inn, you'd be welcome over here, Granville!" Joel patted Barden's shoulder as Scotty scowled.

"Splendid!"

"As long as you can ride like you shoot." Joel quirked his eyebrows.

If this man could shoot like that, would he ride horse like a cowboy?

Or like an outlaw?

Chapter Seven

*T*he kitchen gleamed, all the supper dishes had been put away and the Tumbleston siblings had gone to the town green to listen to some of the soldiers play banjo and some of the other instruments they had.

Barden wiped his hands on one of the towels and then rehung it from its wooden bar. "I'm heading out, Mae." Not to listen to the delightful American music being played, but to practice a western style of riding.

The older woman reached for the bottle of Dr. Williams's Best Liniment, one the Granville's butler swore by. "I think this is helping me. Thank you for having the mercantile order it."

"No trouble at all. Just glad it's helping."

"Between this awful smelling stuff and the chamomile tea, I feel better. Maybe not as good as you young people, but much better than I had been."

He grinned and grabbed his hat from the wall peg. "I'm strolling down to the stables."

Mae cast him a sideways glance. "You don't need to prove anything to those rowdy cowboys out at Martincheks'. From what I've heard, your shooting skills had them swallowing their tongues."

Laughing, Barden nodded at her and took his leave. Outside, the sun was climbing into the beautiful periwinkle blue sky. In future, when he thought of Kansas though, he'd think of Caroline Kane, her hair the color of the blazing sun setting in the west. He'd never get her image out of his mind. And he'd never forget the people. Already, he'd begun to think of them as his flock. He chuckled as he rounded the side of the inn. Luke

Collins sat peeling potatoes, his bad leg supported by him sitting sideways on the bench.

"Good job old fellow. You keep us in eats, don't you?"

The man's shaggy hair flopped down over his eyes. He squinted up. "If I were a full man, like you, I could do so much more."

Barden's eyebrows shot upward but then he trained them back into place. If he was to become a good clergyman he couldn't wear his feelings on his face. Hadn't they taught seminarians how to properly school one's features into a placid expression? "You are a full man. Have you not your soul? Are you not here to fulfill God's purpose for you, yet?"

Oh my, now he was definitely not sounding like an inn worker, much less a cowboy. From Luke's startled expression, Barden knew he'd not said the right thing. He wanted to go ride and learn the proper western seat on a horse, but this man needed him more. Barden sat at the end of the bench and turned toward Collins.

The former soldier exhaled a long puff of air. "Never had another man, other than the preacher, speak to me thataways."

Barden ran his hand over his raspy jawline. With all the work in the kitchen, he'd not taken time for his toilet and he certainly didn't have a valet to assist, like at home.

"Sometimes we need our. . . friend," he was this man's friend, wasn't he? "We need our friends to remind us of things of the eternal. Don't you think?"

"I reckon so."

"Would you tell Mae that she's no longer a woman because of the limitations her earthly body has?"

Collins dropped the potato and knife into the pan. "Never."

"Then why do you speak of yourself in that manner?"

"Dunno."

"If we are to treat others as we would wish to be treated ourselves, why would you not treat yourself with kindness? You are good to others. Can you not be considerate in contemplating yourself?"

His lips pulled in. "When you put it that way, it does sorta make sense."

How Barden wanted to pray with this man. Right here. Right now. But something held him in check. He'd pray for him as he walked. He rose. "I'll be back soon and you let me know if it makes full sense then."

"Sure thing." The new hire resumed peeling potatoes.

As Barden headed down the alleyway he heard Luke whistling. He recognized the tune as "The Ship that Never Returned." Prickles coursed up his arms and to his neck. He paused and listened, trying to remember some of the words to the new song. Was his ship fated to never return? He looked upward to the sky as clouds bundled between the sun and earth, dimming the light. Shaking off foreboding, Barden strode on toward the stables.

As he walked down the boardwalk, he paused to greet some of the inn's customers, giving each an encouraging word. At this rate he'd never get his riding time in.

This is what I made you for.

Barden stopped and glanced around but didn't see anyone who could have spoken to him. A trio of ranch hands rode in, one lifting his hat and the other two nodding in what he could only think of as a respectful acknowledgement. He nodded in return, immediately recognizing it as the curt gesture he'd seen so many times at seminary among his professors. Not the slow nod of respectful acknowledgement. But it was too late now.

Ahead, by the saloon, Melissa Lee and Alan stood glaring at one another.

The couple was supposed to be married soon. They'd been coming into the restaurant regularly for lunch and always loved to chat with him. The Lees owned a prosperous farm out near the Martinchek's ranch. None of the Lee men returned from the war, and Mrs. Lee had died shortly before Barden had arrived, apparently of the same fever that had brought about Mr. Tumbleston's demise.

Mr. Henderson seemed embarrassed that he'd been one of the men who'd auditioned for a bride. But Miss Lee had always reassured him. Never had they seemed angry, as they did now.

"Miss Lee, Mr. Henderson, what's wrong?"

"It's him!" Melissa Lee poked a finger in Alan Henderson's chest.

Henderson captured her hand in his. "It's you and your fool way of thinking."

A dray rolled down the street and paused to turn.

"Why don't we go inside, out of the street?"

"Here?" Miss Lee frowned and looked up at the sagging saloon sign.

Barden fished around in his pocket and opened the door. "We've permission to use it while the army is in town. And they're still here."

He grinned and pointed across to where one of the privates was opening a banjo case.

"All right then." Miss Lee followed him in, trailed by her fiancé.

Henderson gawked at the gaudy interior. "Well don't that beat all? Never seen nothing like this where I come from."

"I should hope not, Alan! A God-fearing man wouldn't be found in a place like this."

"We're here now, aren't we?" Henderson gave his sweetheart a cheeky grin.

Miss Lee crossed her arms over her chest. "That's exactly what I mean. You're always making light of everything I say."

"Everything? I didn't just now."

Barden shook his head and gestured for them to sit in heavy oak chairs nearby at what looked like a gaming table. "All right, how about I ask you a few questions that I believe are basic to any marriage?"

The couple exchanged a long glance.

"What do you say, Melissa?" Henderson raised the pretty brunette's fingers to his lips and kissed them.

She giggled. "Your moustache tickles. But yes, I agree."

"All right then."

"Tell me what you think a God-ordained marriage looks like?"

"God ordained?" Henderson squared his shoulders.

"Yes, for if he's not in your marriage you surely shall have hard times ahead."

Miss Lee tilted her head, a light brown curl trailing down her neck. "I believe in God. And I love Him."

"Me, too." Henderson brushed his fingertips along his cheek. "But I hadn't really thought about what He means in our marriage."

"We go to church regularly." Miss Lee locked eyes with her betrothed.

"Anyone could go into a church." Leaning into the table, Barden steepled his fingers together. "It's what happens in the rest of your life, including in a marriage, which matters."

Henderson's lips pressed into a thin line. "My Ma and Pa said the same thing."

"Well, they were right, weren't they?" Barden squirmed. If he remained much longer he'd never get a chance to ride.

"How about we go for a ride together out into the countryside and let's talk about this." They could do that while he practiced his western seat in the saddle skills.

The two exchanged a glance. "Can't we just keep talking right here?"

Lord, if you needed me in this capacity, you could have kept me in England. Yet He hadn't.

"Indeed. Why not?"

She shouldn't have followed him, but Caroline couldn't resist. The Englishman had shown up in her dreams again last night, this time offering her a lush red rose bouquet and begging her to marry him. She shook her head at the remembrance. Especially since with his gun slinging skills and someone pursuing him, she needed to know more.

Sheriff Ingram lifted his hat as she approached. "Anything wrong, Mrs. Kane?"

Nothing he could fix. It wasn't illegal to steal someone's heart without their consent. "No, thank you."

He was always friendly to her. Poor man had been inundated with females vying for his attention.

"You sure you're all right, Mrs. Kane?"

She needed to find out if Lorraine had spoken with the sheriff about her suspicions. But if she lingered, she'd lose sight of Barden. "Fine. See you!" With that she lifted her skirts, stepped from the boardwalk and after waiting an interminable time for a slow carriage to pass, crossed the street.

Instead of heading to the stables, where he'd said he was going, Barden had stopped to chat with Melissa Lee and Alan Henderson by the saloon.

Keeping close to the shops, she peered through the mercantile's window. With the money from the suitors and from the army, the inn could afford to buy a few things. What was Virginia doing in there? She should be cleaning her room. Her sister bent over a black leather trunk with brass fittings. Poor thing didn't even have a cedar chest. Maybe a trunk like that did make more sense. Especially if she ever obtained a teaching position. Which she didn't currently have. 'Never hurts to look' Mama used to say and Caroline refrained from entering the store.

On the drive back home, the previous day, Barden regaled Caroline with the multitude of reasons that Virginia and Alvin should have a day off. And for them to go scouting out teaching positions for in the autumn. Truth be told, Caroline had been so flustered by the news of someone pursuing Barden and by his shooting skills, to focus very well. He had her more confused than she'd ever been in all her years.

Drawing in a breath of cool late morning air, Caroline continued down the boardwalk. But Barden and her friend were out of sight. She continued on, hoping she'd find them. As she neared the saloon, she heard Melissa's voice raised in anger.

"You do so!"

"I don't." Alan's gruff voice was adamant.

A softer voice interrupted them but she couldn't make out the words. It had to be Barden. She smiled in satisfaction and, glancing around, went around to the side door, opened it, and went in. Carefully she maneuvered behind the elaborate black Chinese fan, located just beside the long bar.

The voices became louder and clearer as she crept closer.

"I think you just want to marry me because of the farm."

"That's part of it."

CARRIE FANCETT PAGELS

"See!" Melissa sounded almost hysterical.

Caroline resisted the urge to charge in and try to help.

"Wait," Barden interrupted. "Let's try establishing a few imperatives for a God-ordained marriage."

What kind of outlaw talked like that? Caroline stiffened. He'd spoken the same way to her. Surely no gunslinging criminal would speak in such a way, would he?

"All right." Melissa sniffed.

"Fine by me."

"Good. First, you have to have committed this upcoming marriage to the Lord. Did you do that?" Barden's deep voice held an authority that she'd not heard before, and she stiffened.

"Of course."

"Not sure what you mean. If we get married won't God bless that?" Alan sounded like such a typical man, which tickled her.

Barden's chuckle matched her own suppressed laugh. Yet even though she knew it was silly to think God would simply bless a union because you stood before a preacher, she'd not sought out God's approval of hers and Barden's upcoming nuptials. Nor had they even spoken of it. Hadn't she been dead set against this whole notion of advertising for a groom, anyways?

"The Almighty wants to be in on everything. Especially in a marriage." Chills coursed down Caroline's arms and she rubbed them.

"I reckon I'd not pondered that much."

"Well you should." Melissa's shrill voice promised another argument.

"Please, you two, yes, you should both seek God's will instead of rushing into a union simply for the sake of having a spouse." Barden sounded remarkably like her father, when he was in one of his sermon moods. But unlike Pa, she decided to not tune Barden out.

"He's not getting just a wife, Mr. Granville, he's getting a farm too."

"How does that factor into your decision, Alan?"

"Well, I ain't gonna lie – it sure don't hurt." Again, his practical, matter-of-fact, response had Caroline holding back a laugh.

"Well, I never!" Melissa huffed.

"It also don't hurt that she's the purtiest gal I've ever laid eyes on."

Caroline peered between the cut-outs on the elaborately carved screen. She spied Alan leaning in to kiss Melissa's cheek, while her pretty friend leaned away from him.

Although she couldn't hear Barden's sigh, she could imagine him doing so. "Those aren't requirements for a marriage. When you enter into holy matrimony you must consider if your love will last through the bad, maybe even the worst, life has to bring."

Barden sounded like he really meant this. He sounded awfully much like a. . . preacher, like he had the previous day. Caroline sucked in a breath.

"Well, I reckon I'd want to marry Melissa and protect her even if she lost that lovely figure of hers and if her pretty face got covered in wrinkles. Preacher, I do know that she's gonna get old one day, just like me. I ain't dumb, even if I am a cowpoke."

Preacher. Alan had called him preacher.

"And I'd still marry Alan if all his beautiful hair fell out." Melissa raised a hand to her mouth and chuckled. "Well, maybe not."

For a moment there was silence. Caroline moved closer. Alan's loud laughter carried, and was joined by the other two's.

"Perhaps the Lord had a reason for sending me here." Barden lowered his head.

"So you really are a priest?" Melissa gasped.

"Don't that mean you can't marry?"

"I'm an Anglican priest. The Church of England allows marriage."

A minister? A crack shot, being tracked down by someone, who'd turned their inn upside down improving it.

Caroline rubbed her head and turned on her heel. There was no way she was going to be able to sort this out by herself.

God was going to have to help. Tears of frustration coursed down her cheeks.

Nothing made sense anymore.

Chapter Eight

Sleep had come in fits and starts for Barden. Caroline had barely spoken to him that previous evening. He awoke early and began his morning in prayer, all the while disturbed in his spirit.

Downstairs, he stopped first in the restaurant, which was empty of all the soldiers, as the others went on into the kitchen. Besides the military and the two traveling Tumblestons something else was absent. Laughter. That was what was missing. Neither Virginia's new-found bright laughter nor Alvin's booming voice carried through the room.

Caroline emerged from the kitchen, tugging at her apron with one hand and carrying a pot of coffee in the other. "Well, Virginia and Alvin set off bright and early. I hope you're happy now."

"Happy?" Indeed, he'd been much happier in America.

"Well, you got your way, didn't you? You wanted them to have time away."

"Caroline, surely you don't begrudge your sister a chance to pursue her dreams?"

When her eyes welled with tears, Barden gently took her hand and led her back through the kitchen, the air heavy with the scent of dough rising, biscuits baking and coffee brewing. Luke grinned up at them as Barden pulled her out the back door. He led her to the bench.

The bright blue sky, dotted with puffs of thin clouds, contrasted with his apprehensive mood. But he'd not let Caroline see that. She dabbed at her eyes with her apron and sat down.

"I don't want to lose Virginia, too."

"I know you don't." Barden squeezed her hand. "But Caroline, your sister is eighteen years old. She's a young woman and God is directing her path toward teaching."

"And she can't teach here. Not unless Birdy marries Drew."

"Right. She had a wonderful teacher with Miss Green, but there is no position at this time." There had been no clergy position in Kent, mainly because Father wanted him far away. He flinched at the memory of learning that fact from the local bishop. Well, right now, he couldn't be much further away. "Miss Green left her a pamphlet about a teacher training and job fair in Topeka."

"Really?" Caroline frowned. "She hasn't said anything to me about it."

Barden exhaled a puff of air. "Perhaps she was waiting until after Leonard's graduation next week, and the army's departure, to make plans."

She sighed. "With all those Army men here, Alvin speaks of nothing else. What will I do if he insists on enlisting?"

"You'll pray. And continue to speak with him about his decisions."

"Father's words fell on deaf ears. If anything, when I caution Alvin, he wants military life even more."

"Either he's going through the normal rebellion of youth or perhaps he, too, is called to the vocation."

"How can you say that?"

"Some men are meant to protect."

"And to abandon their families? Their loved ones?" Caroline narrowed her eyes.

Why was she so angry with him?

She plucked at her cotton apron, forming little folds in the fabric. "At least Luke came back. Why don't you and he go fishing today?"

Why did he sense she wanted him away from her? He stood and feigned removing a hat, then bowed from the waist. "At your service, madam."

If Henry and Leonard behaved like this all summer, maybe she would send them to their grandparents after all. Ever since they'd called out, "We're home!" the two had been at each other, in the kitchen.

Mr. Woodson grabbed a wooden spoon from Mae and aimed it at Henry and Leonard. "I can't abide by fractious children so stop all that bickerin'!"

"It ain't fair that Luke and Barden got to go fishin' when I'm the best around." Henry scowled.

Caroline stopped slicing carrots. "You'll practically be living at the creek the rest of the summer."

Mae cast her a sympathetic look.

Caroline took the spoon from Mr. Woodson and handed it back to Mae. "Henry and Leonard we're sending you on errands and if you're still arguing when you get back then you'll each get to chop wood."

If there was anything the boys hated worse than the kitchen it was chopping wood, stacking it, and bringing it in. They quieted. Then she gave them each a list. "If you fill our list successfully, then you may go fishing."

"Hurrah!" The two boys raced out the door.

Now with Mae, Mr. Woodson, Luke, and Deanna, the large kitchen became hushed.

"Tea anyone?" Caroline went to the tea tin and opened it. Amazing how she'd come to enjoy the beverage so much since Barden had arrived.

Woodson looked up from paring some carrots and shook his head.

Mae smiled up from where she sat kneading bread. "I had mine after we finished cleaning up from lunch."

The clink of a large spoon against the side of a crockery bowl accompanied Deanna's, "Yes, please."

A tray of cookie dough circles, ready to be placed in the oven, bore evidence to Deanna's productivity that afternoon.

"You've certainly earned it." Caroline smiled at Deanna, who averted her gaze. "I've never seen you work so hard."

Suddenly her younger sister burst into tears and then ran outside.

"Better go after her." Mae cast Caroline a sympathetic look.

She found Deanna seated on the bench, head bent over, sobbing into her uplifted apron.

"What's wrong?"

Deanna sniffed, and lifted her face. "They. . .aren't. . ."

"Who?"

"Virginia. . . Alvin." A shuddering sigh shook Deanna's shoulders.

"They aren't what?"

"Coming back." Deanna resumed sobbing.

"What do you mean?"

"They're not coming back here!"

Caroline stiffened. "What do you mean? They're only gone until tomorrow night."

Deanna shook her head hard and then closed her eyes, tears streaming down her face.

Grabbing her sister's arm, Caroline gently squeezed. "Deanna, tell me what you're talking about."

"Army."

"The soldiers left."

Her sister nodded vigorously. "With them."

"Virginia and Alvin went with the army. I knew that, but it's because they were all traveling in the same direction."

"No!"

Dizziness suddenly blurred Caroline's vision as understanding dawned on her. "They intend to go with the army then – to the fort?"

"Alvin is joining the army." Deanna fished a handkerchief out and blew her nose. "I don't know what Virginia intends."

Oh dear. Anger and concern pummeled each other for her attention. "Our sister off with all those men? How could they do that?"

"I'm. . .not sure the captain knows." Deanna wiped her cheeks with her hand. "I should have told you earlier, but Virginia told me not to. She called me a baby and said I spoil all her plans, but you know I don't!"

"It's all right. It's good you told me." Caroline stood, heart hammering. "We've got to go after them."

"I don't know about that. They may hate you if you drag them back here."

Caroline crossed her arms. "Why do you say that?"

"They just want their own lives, Sis, not what Pa wanted for them. Or what you want. Which is basically just what Pa said to do."

What about my heavenly Father? What would He say? Barden was beginning to rub off on her.

"Let's find Barden and ask him to ride after them with Joel and some of his men."

"What if they won't come?" Deanna brushed her tears away.

"We'll have to leave that to Barden and the men to help decide." And to God.

The long ride back, alone, gave Barden new respect for men who spent most of their days in a saddle. But he had nothing to complain about. He'd tried, and he'd failed. But Barden did have a peace about it. Not that he'd blame Caroline for being furious. And hurt. And a multitude of other emotions. Those two siblings had manipulated Barden and lied to Caroline. At least they'd apologized for those two sins. Lorraine, on the other hand, justified her actions, stating that she was the eldest sibling and should be making family decisions.

Sheriff Ingram rode up to him, as Barden neared town. "Just you?"

"Afraid so."

"My wife has been consoling Caroline all afternoon."

"Thank the mayor for me."

"What happened?"

"Those two think they're sufficiently grown up and apparently the army agrees." *And their eldest sister.* Barden ached from head to toe, but mostly he hurt for what this would do to Caroline.

Ingram tipped his hat back. "That boy has been talking of nothing else but soldiering since I met him after arriving in town."

Barden gave a curt laugh. "Mrs. Martinchek signed off for him."

"Did Joel know?"

"Nope." Barden was beginning to sound like a Yank.

"And Virginia?"

"She's offered a teaching position at the fort. And she has a young private besotted with her."

"Sure was good to see that girl smiling these past few days. Wasn't sure she could crack a grin." Sheriff Ingram's eyebrows knit together. "My wife was concerned for her."

"Keep us all in your prayers." *Us.* He had begun to see himself as a part of the Tumbleston family.

"You know it." He wheeled his horse around and accompanied Barden back to the inn, the horse's hooves producing the only sounds.

Town was closed up for the night, with a few shop proprietors straggling home.

The two men split at the alley beside the inn. Barden would take the horse back to the stables after he'd spoken with Caroline. He directed the mare to the trough, dismounted, and tied her to the hitching rail. After taking a few steps onto the boardwalk, he paused at the inn's front door. He surveyed the property and then scanned the street before entering the building, which held the lingering scent of roast pork. His stomach rumbled.

One couple sat at the table in the middle of the room. Birdy Green and her suitor, Drew Cooper. Wouldn't that be something if the two married, leaving the town in need of a teacher after Virginia had already departed? Barden nodded to the couple as he passed. He rubbed his neck.

Woodson stood at the perimeter of the room. "Caroline is upstairs. Mae brought her some more chamomile tea."

Deanna rushed out of the kitchen. She looked at Barden and then beyond. "Where are Virginia and Alvin?"

He shook his head. "Would you kindly request your sister's presence?"

How many stories had this old bench heard? Caroline ran her hand over the dark metal scrollwork, cool to her touch. Barden's handsome face held regret, concern, and something else.

"Thank God my brother and sister are all right." When a tabby cat chased a mouse down the alley, she flinched. "I can't believe they left like that."

"A thousand pardons."

"It's not your fault, Barden." His explanation of what had happened assured her that he'd done all in his power to convince Virginia and Alvin to return, as had the two notes he'd carried with him.

"I wonder, though, why you thought I'd have encouraged such behavior, Caroline?" He rubbed his thumb over the soft flesh of her wrist, distracting her from her sorrow and disappointment. "Not even giving you a fare-thee-well." His brow crinkled and he frowned, leaning forward, elbow on knee.

"For one thing, what you said about following God's will. And that perhaps this was what was right for them."

He straightened. "The other reason?"

"I. . . I heard you with Melissa and Alan yesterday." She nibbled her lower lip.

He frowned. She turned to face him, her skirt pressing against his knees.

Barden's eyes darkened and he leaned toward her, a look of longing coloring his face. How she wished he'd take her in his arms and comfort her.

"I don't see how you could have heard us. We were at the old tavern."

"I snooped." A brave expression fought with her tears as she lifted her chin. "I heard you telling them to have God direct their path and I wondered if you'd told Virginia and Alvin the same thing."

He grasped her hands, his warm and work-chafed. "I'll admit, I may have in one of our conversations."

Caroline tried to tug her hands free, but when he resisted her disengagement she relaxed. "But what if that isn't what's best for them?"

"When wouldn't God's will be best?"

"They're young. They probably don't even know what is best. My father wanted us all together. He wanted me to keep this inn going and to take care of them."

He released her hands and moved closer. She needed his comfort. Never had she felt so forlorn, so distressed.

Barden pulled Caroline into his arms, the softness and warmth of her surging protective desires through him. He tucked her head beneath his chin and patted her back, feeling her ribs beneath the threadbare cloth. She needed more. So much more than he could offer. It was already the middle of June and he would need to depart within a month. How could he leave her now that he loved her so?

"What did you say, Barden?" Caroline pulled back and looked up at him.

Had he uttered the words aloud that groaned in his soul?

He pressed his lips to hers. Yes, he loved her. But he had nothing to offer her. Somehow with her sweet kiss it didn't seem to matter. Barden embraced her and held nothing back as he covered her mouth, her soft cheeks, and her neck with kisses. The scent of sugar and vanilla mixed with floral undertones as he pressed his face into her upswept mass of bright auburn hair. The silky sensation exceeded his wildest imaginations. When he kissed her again, she returned the kiss with fervor and he pulled her closer.

Trying to catch his breath and still his battering heart Barden pulled away. "We must stop."

Caroline blinked up at him, her lips swollen, her breath ragged. She pressed a hand to her bodice.

"I'd never imagined a preacher could kiss like that."

There. She'd reminded him. Had God used Caroline to convict him of the promise he'd already made to the church? "Caroline. . ."

She pressed a finger to his lips. "Don't say anything right now."

Chapter Nine

*C*aroline couldn't repress the smile that kept tugging at her lips all morning. Barden had whispered that he loved her. And the thrill of his kisses had traveled clear down to her laced-up boots. She unlocked the front door of the restaurant and then opened the gingham curtains. The windowpanes sparkled thanks to Barden's and the boys' efforts. Without Virginia there, she now had to make sure the restaurant was ready to receive diners in the morning. Since only ten inn guests slept upstairs, it should be a fairly slow morning.

God, please watch over Virginia and Alvin. And may the Lord help her forgive the way they departed.

After tying back the last curtain she strained to look out at the street, where a trio of men rode into town. Peculiar how they seemed to lift slightly from their saddles. That was the same manner in which Barden rode. Unease dribbled through her like hot sorghum syrup on pancakes, especially when one of the men pointed toward the inn.

Caroline hurried to the back and called to Deanna. "I think we have customers."

Mae glanced up from cracking eggs into a bowl. "We'll be ready. Barden has coffee going and the biscuits are baked."

Barden swiveled away from the stove and winked at her, sending her heart skittering down some happy lane where she longed to go. "Deanna will be down in a moment—had some distress with her ribbons."

"Probably slept with them in her hair again." Tugging at her apron until it was perfectly straight and the ruffles aligned,

Caroline headed back out to the restaurant as the front door swung in.

The first two men removed their tan dusters and handed them to the third man, who carried them back out the door. *Odd.*

"May I help you?"

The taller of the two men, with silvery mutton-chop whiskers, turned to the other man, whose round face was cleanly shaven. "Let's partake of breakfast first, eh, before seeking out the lad?"

The man's British accent was thicker than Barden's yet also crisper, as if this was a man used to being in command.

"Capitol idea."

This wasn't the capital but it would be rude to correct the man. Caroline gestured toward the center table. No guests from upstairs had yet come down. "You have the place to yourselves, gentlemen."

"Jolly good." He didn't look jolly at all, as a frown formed between his white eyebrows.

"What are you serving, this morn, madam?" The round-faced man's ruddy cheeks sported a hint of missed whiskers, a sign of haphazard shaving.

"Fried potatoes, ham, scrambled eggs, and biscuits with gravy." Pretty much the same most days. "And coffee."

"Tea?"

"Yes." Only since Barden had arrived.

"Marvelous. We'll start with a pot of tea and take all the rest of the breakfast offerings."

The third, and younger man, reentered the building. The two dusters now appeared a shade lighter in color so he must have beaten the dust from them and from his own jacket, which he'd removed. He hung each one on a peg before wiping his hands. He turned toward her. "Do you have a water closet on this floor, miss?"

"Water closet? Oh, we do have a wash bowl, soap, and water in that room beneath the stairs." She pointed to the back.

"Much obliged." Although his response was a typical cowboy thank you, the man's intonation was a more guttural version of Barden's accent.

Caroline gestured toward the younger man as he headed back. "Will he be joining you?"

"Jonathan will want his own table." The dark-haired man pointed to the far wall. "And a newspaper if you've one handy."

"Last week's Kansas Collective is here."

The older gentleman arched an eyebrow. "That'll do."

"Will he want tea?" She thought she should ask. But what kind of cowboys ordered tea? Thick black coffee was their lifeblood.

"Indeed, and plenty of sugar."

"I'll have everything out shortly."

A niggling feeling continued in her stomach as Caroline headed to the kitchen where Mae, Mr. Woodson, and Leonard were working. "Where's Barden?"

Leonard gestured out back.

Deanna walked in, her hair covered in some kind of turban. It wasn't worth asking about.

"Deanna, I need three breakfast plates brought out, please."

After grabbing a tray, Caroline placed the sugar bowl, three cups, three small plates, and a basket of biscuits atop. Then she took one of the butter crocks and set a knife on it before retrieving utensils and napkins.

"Coffee?" Mr. Woodson hoisted the pot aloft.

"No, I'll need tea. Make enough for three men."

Mae's eyes widened. "Who are they?"

"They're English but they look like ranchers."

The back door swung open as Barden carried in a basketful of wood for the stove.

Her heart skipped a beat as her lips burned with the memory of the previous night's kiss. Barden's eyes locked on hers and his cheeks reddened. He'd said he loved her. And if thinking of him all the time, dreaming about him, and feeling like her world had turned upside down was love, then she, too, loved him. But this was such a different kind of love than she'd had with Frank. She was falling in love with her own fiancé. Except that Barden never actually spoken to her about marriage—only the future. Were these Englishmen here about him?

"You all right, Mrs. Kane?" Barden's dark blond hair fell forward and he brushed it back.

Mrs. Kane, *not* Caroline. But when he smiled at her, her heart wobbled in her chest.

Everyone returned to their work. Barden patted his vest pocket. "I almost forgot—I have a letter that Mrs. Freeman sent for you."

"I've got to serve these men and I'll be right back." She didn't want to stay, afraid of what Barden might tell her. But there were many British ranchers in the west. "They're Englishmen."

"Oh?" His voice sounded strained. "Did you catch their names?"

"No. They seem quite focused on getting their food."

"Ah. Very good." But his light brows drew together and he turned away from her.

As Caroline carried the heavy tray out to the table, her unease built. First she served the two men at the table.

"We're strangers in town as I imagine you've discerned." The younger of the two men opened his napkin and laid it across his lap.

She couldn't help the smile that tugged at her lips. "I figured as much."

"We're looking for my godson." The older man's voice took on a formal tone. "Barden Granville IV, the son of our good friend, Lord Cheatham."

Thank goodness her tray had been considerably lightened or the tremor in her hands would have toppled everything onto the men.

What the men said didn't make sense. Why did Barden have a different last name from his father? Was he an illegitimate son? Was he hiding in America? If so, why would these two men be seeking him out?

"Uncle Drayton!" Barden called out from behind her.

Caroline turned and set the tray on the adjacent table.

"Good to see you old chap."

When the men didn't rise, Barden bent and hugged Mr. Drayton and then straightened and shook hands with the other man. Caroline headed over to check on the third guest.

"Sorry it took so long, old chap, but we're here now." Uncle Drayton leaned back in his chair and gestured to the seat adjacent him. "Have a sit down."

Barden raised his hands. "I'm afraid I can't. I've work to do."

The two men exchanged a glance and Chesterfield guffawed. "You've taken over a Church of England parish here, then lad?"

"That's a good one." Drayton laughed.

Not a bad idea, now that they mentioned it. The nondenominational church he attended with Caroline was shepherded by a frail elderly minister. And the reverend had recently confided that he wished to return back east. "No. I am employed here at the inn."

"Here?" Drayton pressed a hand to his chest.

The younger man, in the corner, glanced their way as Caroline left his table, her shoulders stiff. What had his uncle's valet told her? Hopefully he maintained the same level of discretion as he did in England. But Barden had changed since leaving. What he used to think of as proper or refined seemed superfluous and a way of avoiding dealing with feelings. On the other hand, the gentleman cowboy he'd read of in his dime novels, seemed scarcer than a farthing in these parts.

"We received some news from your father just before we left." Drayton steepled his fingers together. "Seems you are to be an uncle soon."

"Excellent." Barden could imagine the delight his brother would have. Granted the future Earl of Cheatham's happiness would be tenfold if his wife produced an heir.

"But Peter. . ." Lord Chesterfield's pronunciation, like Barden's own, drew out his brother's name and omitted the 'r' sound, unlike the Americans did. "Has taken ill with a cough."

Uncle Drayton waved a hand dismissively but the tension in his features belied his casual gesture. "Don't worry yourself. You're going home. You'll see him soon."

"And Father?" The physician had said it would be only a matter of time before his heart condition worsened.

The two men exchanged a glance.

"See what you make of the missive he sent." Chesterfield was as pragmatic as ever.

"Must have had his valet write it. Cheatham's handwriting always was atrocious."

Barden's voice seemed stuck in his throat. "Was he too ill to write it himself?" Too weak?

"Apparently he was too distressed about his missing son to write the letter." Drayton's tone held a bite of accusation.

"Maybe I am the Prodigal Son after all." Shame brought heat to Barden's face. He swiped a hand across his cheek.

"Tut-tut. We've sent a transatlantic cable to London to be delivered to him." Chesterfield tapped his thick fingers atop the table. The last time Barden had seen the man, he'd been dressed for dinner in his finest attire, the table covered with layers of starched linen tablecloths, all the silver on display, the crystal gleaming, and the early 18th century French china shining at his country estate.

"If it gets through." Which Barden doubted.

Chesterfield lifted his double chin. "There have been vast improvements now and by all reports this attempt at the telegraph cable is expected to succeed."

"Regardless, we've also dispatched a letter to him. And we indicated we'd get you home post haste." Had Drayton's long thin nose always seemed raised so high?

Barden splayed his hands. "But I'm not ready to leave." He loved his father but he'd been preparing him for years to be an independent thinker and to always weigh matters. "Did he request my presence at home?"

"No," Drayton grudgingly admitted. "He seemed more bent on getting some word from you."

Uncle Drayton opened a small leather bag that hung from his neck by rawhide. How incongruous to see this man, the son of a peer, dressed not in silks and ready for the *ton* but with skin

CARRIE FANCETT PAGELS

dark as rawhide, attired in a cotton shirt and dungarees. Granted, his clothing was perfectly tailored to his build and he still sported a white cravat at his neck instead of a handkerchief. "Here you go." He passed Barden the envelope.

Barden recognized the handwriting immediately and he exhaled in relief. "This is Mother's script."

"Not in the habit of corresponding with her, I dare say." His father's friend raised his bushy eyebrows high.

Barden jabbed at the bottom. Unlike the rest of her handwriting, Mother's signature was, as usual, indecipherable and next to it she'd carefully written Father's name. "She probably asked Father to write you and when he refused, she took it upon herself to do so. Which means he wasn't expecting to hear anything from me until I arrived back in England to assume the vicarage."

"Mother's intuition, my boy." Chesterfield had a half dozen sons, four of whom had traveled with him to America.

"Indeed." Drayton had left his wife across the ocean, as well as his children.

Chesterfield's eyes gleamed. "So. Will you rush home to England?"

Trying not to eavesdrop, Caroline sought to focus on Jonathan, presumably one of these men's servants. She couldn't help watching the others from the corner. Bits and pieces of her British novels flew at her. An aristocrat often went by the name of his estate but would have a different surname. So perhaps that was Barden's father's case. Which meant that Barden was the son of a British nobleman.

"You all right miss?" The young man cocked his head at her. "You look like you've witnessed something skilamalink."

She blinked at him.

"Sorry miss. You look like you can't believe your eyes. I think that's the expression." Jonathan was a handsome man and his grin might have sent flutters through someone else but in her current state she simply wanted to collapse out of view and cover her face with her apron.

But she couldn't waste this chance to find out more about Barden and these strangers. "I'm fine. I. . . I forgot to bring the gravy."

He laughed as he slathered butter on his biscuit and reached for the strawberry preserves. "Don't bother yourself, miss. That'd be like butter upon bacon."

"So sorry, I don't have bacon today, simply ham."

Again he chuckled. "I meant no need for gravy for me, this is fine."

Barden tilted his head toward them and paused in his conversation. Was that her imagination or did his narrowed eyes look jealous? She patted the curl that trailed over her shoulder. She leaned in closer. "What brings you gentlemen out to Turtle Creek?"

"Bringing money to old Bardy to get him home again."

From Barden's table, she caught the words of the one gentleman asking if Barden would be going there, which reaffirmed this man's words. Dizziness washed over her, but Caroline forced herself to keep breathing.

"You sure you're all right, miss?"

She positioned her back to Barden, who had not only concealed his background but that he planned only to swoop in here, steal her heart and then run back to England. All with not so much as a fare thee well—just like he'd accused her siblings of doing.

"What's that, miss? Fare thee well?"

Now she was even picking up Barden's recent habit of talking under his breath. She poured a cup of tea for him, her hands trembling. "Oh, sorry, I meant he'll need a fare as well, won't he? On a ship."

Jonathan gave her a sharp look. "I'm not openin' my sauce-box about all that."

"Sauce box?"

He pointed to his mouth. "Not my place to comment even if Lord Cheatham is a right old. . ." He glanced toward the others. "Cheatham ain't like them at all. They're what you call real gents."

CARRIE FANCETT PAGELS

Jonathan shoved half a biscuit in his mouth and Caroline retreated to the kitchen.

She grabbed the Freemans' missive from the counter and then strode out the back and around to the side, to Mama's bench. She sank onto it, arranging her skirts around her. Unfolding the light tan paper, she read Mary's flowing script.

Caroline, How we miss you, girl! God bless you for all you done for us. And we pray Barden has brought the help your father thought you'd need after he died. I'm sorry we took so long findin someone. We got busy and plum forgot about your father's request to place the ad for him. But when Barden came to us, we thought God had provided. So we sent him on. We're sorry he can't stay too long with you, but we pray he's been of help this summer.

The letter fell into her lap. *He can't stay too long.*

This was all a misunderstanding. She pressed her fingers to her lips. That kiss was no misunderstanding. Those kisses had been full of passion that had bespoke marital commitment. Heat singed her cheeks at the recollection.

He'd just been toying with her affections.

And soon he'd be gone. Back to his father.

Chapter Ten

*T*ears streamed down Caroline's face, unimpeded, as she strode through the grassy field to the cemetery. If Pa were here, she'd tell him all about it. She would have talked with Mae, but the older woman seemed so taken with Barden.

How were Alvin and Virginia doing, on their way to Fort Mackinac? Barden had come into their lives and had shaken things up. But Lorraine had been trying to do that for so long, that it was as if Barden had simply taken over her job. No, it wasn't like that. She sniffed. And she knew Lorraine meant well, in her own meddling way.

Caroline strode to her father's grave and sank down onto her knees. *This is so hard. I was just getting used to the notion that I might be able to run the inn by myself.*

You have never been alone. That assurance came from God. Her earthly father may be gone, but her heavenly Father still remained.

God, I don't know what to do with all these feelings. She let out a sob that grew into a moan. She'd not grieved her father but with the upcoming loss of Barden, who'd not been a husband candidate after all, the dam burst loose inside her. Bending over, she raised her apron to her eyes and caught the tears that should have been shed months ago.

You left me. You left us. You, Frank, and Ma are gone. Caroline glanced to her parents' headstone and then beyond, several rows, to Frank's.

Birdsong carried from nearby stands of willows. Their cheerful tweets and warbles seemed so at odds with the painful stuttering of her heart.

Why me, God? Why this pain?

Because she'd finally opened herself up to real love. Not a safe love—one that her friend, her husband, had sought to leave almost as soon as they were wed. He'd confessed as much during his fevered state.

She sniffed.

Real love means wanting what was best for the other person.

Barden was a priest. He'd said so. Which meant he had a flock to tend to in England. She swiped her eyes with her sleeve.

Caroline fished her handkerchief out of her pocket. Anger burned within her. How dare Barden make her fall in love with him? Tears began anew. Now she was really becoming ridiculous. She hiccupped a laugh at herself as she walked back to the inn.

How she wished to go back to her room and have a good long rest. Caroline rubbed the side of her aching head. Both Leonard and Deanna had sat in her bedroom with her into the late hours, sharing how they missed Pa and now Virginia and Alvin. They'd launched into a reverie about Frank and about Ma, too. When they'd begun discussing whether they should reconsider their grandparents' offer of a train ticket, Caroline had finally sent them off to bed. She'd told them, "If I let you two travel across country you'd both kill each other before you ever arrived."

The two, for some reason, could not resist teasing one another, poking one another, and in general bedeviling one another's lives. Yet they were still grieving, like she was. And they rose each morning to help, instead of running off to the creek or to a friend's home, or a quilting bee. Tears pricked her eyes. They were a blessing and she was failing them. If only she could rest. Then she'd think more clearly.

When she reached the inn, she walked around to the right and up the alley, entering through the back door.

Mae looked up from where she was transferring strawberry jam from a large crock into smaller dishes. "The evening coach should arrive soon."

The quilts atop Caroline's bed seemed to be calling for her to return.

"What is on the lunch menu today?" Barden joined them and stood at the counter, drying glasses as Mr. Woodson washed and rinsed them.

"Whatever Deanna and Henry cook," she retorted. Barden would be leaving soon. The others needed to get accustomed to cooking again.

Mrs. Reed chuckled. "I've yet to see them prepare an entire meal."

Eying the pot of leftover beans and the biscuits nearby, Caroline shrugged. "They can throw some ham on the stove and serve that with the beans."

Blonde eyebrows inched upward as Barden blinked at her. "Surely you don't intend to inflict that slop upon your guests."

Planting her hands on her navy calico-covered hips, Caroline stared at him. She was too weary to argue. "You have any better ideas? Because I'm going upstairs for a lie down."

"You do that, dear." Mae nodded at her. "You look worn to the bone."

When tears threatened to spill, Caroline swiveled on her heel and headed to the stairs.

Leonard, stirring the mashed potatoes, chewed on his lower lip and frowned. "Sis never naps this long."

A niggling sensation began in Barden's spirit. "I sent Deanna up several minutes ago to check on her."

"Dinner's gonna get cold." Henry lifted the cover and peeked into the pan of pork chops that Barden had fried.

Father's friends and their servant had chosen to rest and had gone up to nap earlier.

Deanna, face flushed, bounded into the kitchen. "She's not waking up."

"What do you mean?" Barden narrowed his eyes at Deanna. "Could you not rouse her?"

"I wouldn't slap her awake or anything."

"Nor would I wish you to do so."

Mrs. Reed removed her checkered apron. "Let me go check. You all go ahead, sit down and eat your supper."

"I'm coming, too." Barden followed the older woman.

Mrs. Reed grabbed one of the stairway lamps and held it aloft. When they reached the upper level, Barden heard footsteps thundering up. He turned to see pools of lamplight illuminating the stair treads as Henry and Leonard pounded up to the landing.

Mrs. Reed turned and scowled. "Well if she was asleep and just resting, she'll certainly be awake now."

"Sorry." The two mumbled.

The older woman rolled her eyes, slowly swiveled around and went to Caroline's door. She held the lamp aloft. Even from this distance, Barden could see that her long auburn hair was darkened and damp with fevered perspiration.

Mrs. Reed pressed a hand to Caroline's brow. "Caroline, do you hear me?"

There was no response.

The boys elbowed in past Barden, whose breath stuck in his throat.

"Get the doctor." Leonard barked the order at his younger brother and Barden flinched.

Henry went to the door. "We ain't waiting."

Leonard wiped a tear from his eye as his younger brother departed. "Sorry. I shouldn't have yelled."

"It's all right. You've been through a lot. Too much." Mae gave the boy a quick hug. "I'll get some cool water and prepare willow bark tea while you get Doc."

"I'll stay." Barden pulled the lone chair in the room closer to the bedside, as Mae lit another lamp for him and set it on the side table.

"I'll wait with Sis." Leonard placed his hand possessively on the chairback.

"No, it's my pleasure." Not quite a pleasure but not a duty either. The only thing Caroline and he had connecting them was a nascent love—but oh how that love was beginning to flame.

Mrs. Reed paused in the doorway. "This is just how Frank died, poor dear. And there was nothing Caroline could do for him."

A sick feeling swelled in his gut as Barden bent over the bed and Leonard slunk into the chair.

"Water?" Caroline's raspy voice jarred Barden awake.

How long ago had he nodded off since he'd displaced Leonard in the chair? He rose, his legs stiff from being bent in place so long. "Coming."

He adjusted the lamp's wick higher, the light illuminating Caroline's hair, strewn across her pillow like strands of molten copper.

"Water."

His hands shook as he lifted the blue and white pitcher. He poured a matching cup half full and then set it and the carafe atop the bedside table. "Let me help you sit up first."

Gently he lifted Caroline's head, which still burned with fever. He gathered the pillows, plumped them and then placed them beneath her shoulders.

"Thank you." Her voice was low and strained.

"You are most welcome." He turned and grabbed the water and then pressed it into her hands. She wrapped both around the cup before raising it to her lips. Sweat glistened on her beautiful face.

"What time is it?"

He pulled out his pocket watch, which he still had set to Greenwich Time. Calculating the difference from that and what the locals in this town used, he arrived at a number. "About two in the morning."

Caroline handed him back the water and pushed her head back into the pillows. "When will you go?"

"Go?"

"Home."

He took her hand in his. Hot and limp, she barely squeezed his fingers in return. "I don't know."

She shuddered out a sigh. "Sorry."

"For what?"

"I thought. . ."

"I'm sorry, too. I didn't realize, but I should have." He'd walked right in upon the auditions of the town women. She'd not participated in the event. "And I should have told you why I'd come to America."

"Cowboy?"

"Yes." He leaned in and kissed her forehead. "You need to get well so we can make a proper cowgirl of you."

"Indian maiden."

"Ah, those are some of my favorite stories but you are entirely too fair for that."

"Cowboy preacher?"

Not a bad idea.

In the stupor she fought against, Caroline could barely manage to speak. "Love you." Barden's parishioners would love him regardless of whether he showed up in clerical garb or in cowboy clothes with a lasso.

"I love you, too." He pressed a kiss to her hand.

Comfort at having him near pulsed through her.

"They need you." Barden had people waiting on his return. "Your church."

"I need you more." His raspy voice seared something inside her.

"Go." She had to let him go and fulfill his promise.

Through her half-opened eyes she saw him frown. "Go get Deanna and the boys? Please don't leave us, my love."

"No." She couldn't be alone. Not with the way she felt. This tugging, this pulling of something carrying her like an ocean pulling her out into a hot sea. "Don't. . .leave me."

"I won't." Barden sat down next to her on the bed, gently pressing his lips to her cheek.

You're never alone. The words were spoken into her heart. Caroline sensed the presence of others in the room, but she couldn't see them, although she knew they beckoned her on.

I want to stay. Let me stay for Barden.

Barden's own footfall rumbled down the stairs even louder than the boys' had thundered up the night before. He rushed into the kitchen. "Her fever has broken!"

He swept Mrs. Reed into his arms and twirled the woman around.

Mr. Woodson ceased stirring the potatoes he was frying in the skillet. "Glory be!"

Deanna rushed into his arms just as Barden released Mrs. Reed.

"You really love Caroline, don't you?" Deanna's eyes took on the dreamy gaze he'd often seen in females enthralled with the notion of romance.

"Yes, I care deeply for your sister."

"And I can tell she loves you, too."

She did. He knew it in his very being. "I believe so."

"So when ya gonna get hitched then?"

"Hitched? You mean married?" He lowered his head. *What are your plans, Lord?*

"Ain't that what you came here to Turtle Creek for?" Woodson began pushing the potatoes around in the frying pan again.

"Actually, no. I came here at the behest of the Freemans."

"Mary and Uziah?" Deanna raised her eyebrows.

"The Freemans felt I could help with the work here."

"So you weren't here for the auditions?" The girl tossed her braid over her shoulder and backed up. "Whew! Good thing we listened to Sis and didn't tease you about being a mail-order groom!"

"No. I'm afraid I was here on a bit of a jaunt. Thought myself a holiday cowboy—but that didn't work out."

Now what to do about my obligations. "I'm ordained by the Church of England. . ."

"You ain't in England, anymore." Woodson turned and locked gazes on him. "In case you haven't noticed."

"I have taken note. In the meanwhile, I have a hungry inn owner upstairs for whom I'm the very willing footman. What do you have for me to take upstairs?" To the woman he couldn't live without.

Chapter Eleven

Late June, 1866

*D*espite the drizzle, Caroline sat outside on the bench, an umbrella held overhead, and pillows propped around her. After being abed for over a week, recovering, the fresh cool air lifted her spirits as did the scent of roses nearby.

Someone turned the corner into the alleyway. Steel gray hair curled beneath a bowler hat as a stranger strolled toward her. The powerfully built man must have been a fearsome sight when he was younger, but as he neared, his kind dark eyes urged Caroline to welcome him.

He removed his hat and tucked it under his suited arm, despite the rain's increase. "Are you the inn's owner?" The man's accent was heavy, but much different from Barden's, with a roll to it and unlike Barden's clipped tones. "Are you Mrs. Kane?"

"Yes, I am."

"I'm looking for. . . a friend."

Movement from behind her caught her attention. Head down, Barden rounded the corner, wiping his hands on a dish towel, surged toward them. "Good heavens, woman, it is raining out here. You'll catch your death yet!"

Her beloved almost reached her when he stopped.

The stranger beamed at Barden. "Mr. Granville, I am here."

"Sinclair!" Barden opened his arms and the two embraced each other like long last friends. "What are you doing here?"

"It's a rather convoluted tale, but. . ."

"Let me get this misbehaving lady inside before you tell me all."

"I'm simply enjoying the day outside." As Caroline rose, she swayed and Barden caught her. He lifted her into his arms.

"What did I tell you, Caroline?" He shifted her weight, the scent of his clove shaving soap teasing her senses. "Don't push yourself."

Mr. Sinclair cocked his head. "Have you been ill, Mrs. Kane?"

"Indeed she has, we could have lost her. But praise be to God she's with us yet."

Sinclair glanced between the two of them, his brown eyes seeming to take in everything. He followed them into the kitchen and then on to the restaurant, where Barden finally lowered her into a chair.

"Thank you." She'd love to thank him with a kiss, but words would have to do—for now.

"Sinclair was my manservant, in England, Caroline."

Mr. Sinclair patted moisture from his face with a creamy handkerchief. "Was is the operative word. Lord Cheatham wasn't at all pleased when he'd learned I'd encouraged your interest in the Beadle's books. Nor that I knew you'd taken holiday in America to try your hand at cowboy life."

"Outrageous!" Barden's face twisted in an anger she'd never seen before. "How could Father simply dismiss you?"

Bowing his head briefly, Barden leaned against the back of his sweetheart's chair. His little cowboy venture had cost his valet his position. "How did you get here, Sinclair?"

"I came in my voyage to search for you, sir, to ensure that you were well. I didn't hear from you after that message from your hotel."

"After I was attacked. . ."

A muscle in his valet's jaw twitched. "If only I had been here to help you."

Barden motioned for his friend to sit. "You're here now. How did that happen since my father sacked you?"

"I'd put aside funds for my old age, and I appear to be in it now."

"You're hardly in your dotage." Barden laughed. "In fact you look to be in remarkably good condition."

Sinclair patted his midsection. "American food agrees well with me thus far."

Mrs. Reed wheeled the tea cart in. "I understand we have guests."

"Indeed." Barden waved a hand toward his former servant. "May I introduce John Sinclair, an old and dear friend."

Sinclair shot him a look of gratitude. "And responsible for him taking this lark by coming to America and scaring the wits out of us back home."

Mrs. Reed's cheeks flushed. Was she blushing? "What will you do here, Mr. Sinclair?"

"I'm hoping to go for a land grant." Sinclair's cheeks, too, took on a rosy hue. "Perhaps out here or back further east."

Caroline leaned in, resting her elbows on the table. "To become a farmer?"

"Own my own bit of land. My father was a tenant farmer. I only took up the life in service when we'd had two droughts back-to-back."

"I see." Mrs. Reed's wide eyes seemed to be taking in much.

"I met your friends, the Freemans." Sinclair rapped his fingers on the table. "Good people."

"Indeed. They saved me." *In more ways than one.* He gazed at Caroline. What would life have been like without her in it?

Mrs. Reed served them each tea, her hands a bit unsteady as she poured for Sinclair. Thank God her rheumatism had improved enough for her to hold and tip a tea pot again.

"Thank you, madam." Sinclair's dark eyes took on a gleam as he looked up at Mrs. Reed.

"Call me Mae."

"Delighted to do so." Sinclair gave her a cheeky grin.

Caroline turned to Barden. "Take a seat."

After pouring in milk, Sinclair used the sugar tongs to drop two chunks of sugar into his tea.

"I should have let you pour your milk first, like Barden does." Mrs. Reed blinked down at Sinclair.

As Barden settled into his chair, Caroline beamed up at him, her face still wan but just as beautiful. Thank God she'd soon fully regain her health.

"No trouble at all. Thank you." Sinclair drew in a deep breath, exhaled, and fixed his gaze on Barden. "I have a bit of news I felt you should hear directly from me, since it is my fault you are here."

Barden sipped his tea, eyeing Sinclair over the top of his teacup. "What might that be?"

"The parish has rescinded their offer of a position."

He gulped the hot tea, almost choking on it. "What?"

"When your father heard what you had done, he wrote to the bishop and told them he wouldn't sponsor the living for you."

Ire rose up but was quickly chased by confusion and then relief. "I never realized Father had anything to do with the position since it was so far from home."

"Yes, that horrid man. . ." Sinclair raised his hand and then lowered it. "My apologies, but he never deserved a good son like you."

And Barden had never deserved a companion as faithful as John Sinclair. A man who would follow him across the ocean to check on him. Who was a better father to him than his own had been.

Caroline laughed. "I guess you don't have to write that letter to them after all, do you, Barden?"

Squeezing her hand, Barden leaned closer to the woman he'd spend the rest of his life with. "But, what then shall I do?"

Caroline cocked her head at him. "Besides marry me?"

"Have you decided?" Barden chuckled. "I believe you hired me on a temporary basis but now I understand you had something else in mind."

The door to the inn opened. Caroline turned as the mayor and her husband, the sheriff, entered; trailed by Melissa and Alan and the preacher.

"We're married!" Melissa, dressed in a pretty pink dress with lace-edged flounces, moved past the others to Caroline's table. "I'm Mrs. Henderson now."

Barden and Mr. Sinclair stood.

"Congratulations!" Caroline grinned up at her pal.

Her friend pressed a quick kiss to Caroline's cheek. "How're you feeling?"

Barden cleared his throat. "She's going back upstairs to rest soon. Congratulations on your wedding."

Reverend Smith nodded to them. "You still going to substitute for me next Sunday, when I visit my daughters?"

"Yes, sir."

"I assume you won't be utilizing the Book of Common Prayer." Sinclair's droll expression made Barden chuckle.

"No, indeed."

Sheriff Ingram moved forward and shook Barden's hand. "Think about my offer, too."

Caroline narrowed her eyes at him, in question.

Mrs. Reed tapped his shoulder. "Would you like me to pull these tables together?"

Instead of a country parish council meeting, Barden found himself in Kansas surrounded by people trying to put their village back together again after a terrible civil war.

And he had perfect peace that this was where he belonged.

After Caroline had awoken from her nap, Barden brought her to the saloon, protectively steadying her on the boardwalk.

"I want to show you what I was telling the mayor about, before you nodded off earlier." He ran his thumb over her chin, sending a delicious thrill through her. "I should have carried you up to bed sooner."

Her cheeks heated. Very soon they'd be married and would share a bed. She took a step away from him and scanned the saloon's main floor, spotless and serene—so unlike the place had been when formerly occupied.

Barden squared his shoulders. "Can you imagine your American veterans coming to a place where they could not only recover from the ravages of war but be retrained?"

"Mayor Ingram says we need more men, more businesses. Why not try?"

"I hope she's right, that the council might donate the building."

"If not, perhaps there's another way." Upstairs, in her room, was a bank check that Barden's rancher friends had sent as a wedding gift. They were off on a cattle drive and wouldn't make it back for the nuptials. Nor would Alvin and Virginia be there to attend but the Freemans would.

She took two steps toward him and pressed her hands against his chest. "With more people coming to Turtle Creek, the sheriff said he might need a deputy."

"I'm a good shot." He grinned. "But Caroline, I did not pursue ministry simply because I was never going to be Lord Cheatham. I want God to direct my path."

She leaned her head against him, and he tucked his chin down. "Do you think supplying for Reverend Smith will be enough?"

"I'm not sure. But if I can meet the needs of men, like those who came through here and headed off to the fort, and men like Luke Collins, then I'll have served well."

Caroline snuggled in, turning her head, listening to his heart beat out a steady booming rhythm. "You're a blessing to everyone who comes through the inn."

Barden stepped back. "I don't know what I'll be doing for certain, my love, but I do know that wherever and whatever I am doing I want you there by my side."

"How about in your arms?" Caroline grinned up at her fiancé, and moved closer, lifting her face up for a kiss.

Barden's lips covered hers.

Mail-order husband or not, this Englishman's heart belonged to her.

Epilogue

October, 1866

*B*arden clutched his mother's letter so hard that it crumpled. Father's heart had finally given out. Poor Peter's wife had lost their baby and then the new Earl of Cheatham had taken ill with pneumonia. *Lord help them all.* Barden trusted God to get him through whatever life threw at him. Today, though, he would share nothing of Mother's letter with Caroline. This was their wedding day and there was nothing they could do for Father. He'd do nothing to ruin this day.

Someone knocked on the door.

"Yes?"

"Sinclair, sir, may I enter?"

He grinned. "Certainly." No need to share Mother's words with this dear man, either. He'd tell Sinclair later.

Sinclair entered and dipped his chin. "Might I assist you?"

Barden gestured to the wedding suit he'd donned. "I think I'm all set."

Sinclair patted his breast pocket. "I've got the ring."

"Splendid."

A grin crept across the older man's face. "I expect I'll be purchasing a wedding suit for myself very soon."

Barden clapped his friend on the shoulder. "So Mae said 'yes'?"

He nodded.

"Look what you and all those dime novel cowboy stories have resulted in, Sinclair."

"I'd say blessings upon blessings, sir."

"I agree."

This autumn was surely bringing her a harvest of blessings. Deanna patted Caroline's hair, which Lorraine had swept up into a fancy chignon with jeweled hairpins.

"You look beautiful." Lorraine, attired in a lovely double-skirted blue and green gown with a triangular bodice, beamed her approval.

Deanna wore a turquoise gown that complemented Lorraine's, courtesy of Barden. "Aren't my fancy Pagoda sleeves fashionable?"

Lorraine raised her eyebrows. "They may be, but you're too young for that off-the-shoulder style, even if it is the fashion."

Caroline resisted the urge to sigh, not wanting anything to spoil her wedding day.

"I'm not too young." Her lips formed a pout. "Virginia says the ladies at Fort Mackinac wear their dresses this way."

"I'm thrilled that Virginia is so happy on Mackinac Island." But Virginia's request that Deanna join her this spring concerned Caroline.

A double rap at the door sounded before Melissa Henderson slipped into the room. "Oh, my, I don't want to crowd you sisters but I wanted to let you know your carriage is ready."

"Oooh, that sounds so fancy—like Barden has become Lord Cheatham and is about to make our sister Lady Caroline." Deanna dipped a curtsey.

All eyes locked on Deanna as Caroline and the other two gaped at the girl.

"What?" Deanna shrugged. "What did I say wrong?"

"For one thing, his father and brothers would have to die for that to happen." Lorraine rolled her eyes heavenward.

Deanna's hands flew to her mouth, and her cheeks reddened. "I didn't mean that at all. I was just—"

Caroline splayed her fingers in front of her. "Let's forget that. It's okay, Deanna." She patted her hair and tried to change the subject. "Thank you Lorraine and Deanna for all your help and how lovely my hair looks, too!"

All three women visibly relaxed. Melissa gave her a smile of approval at her distraction technique—one her friend often used herself.

"So are you ready?" Melissa cocked her head as if examining Caroline.

"To become Mrs. Barden Granville?" Lorraine pulled at Caroline's full elliptical skirt and gestured for her to turn. "Lovely."

"Let me adjust that bow on the back." Deanna yanked and twisted the material.

Melissa joined them and gently pulled the skirt's vibrant green silk fabric out more fully. "Gowns certainly are getting more expansive in the back, aren't they?"

"You certainly look like a lady even if that's not your title." Deanna apparently couldn't let that topic go.

Still, a chill slid down her arms. They were to travel to England in the in springtime. She'd meet Barden's family. She had the strangest sensation, maybe a God whisper, that her world was about to change immensely. This did not feel like wedding jitters.

But how would she know how to be a proper lady? She wouldn't. But that would still be all right.

Regardless. . . "All that matters is that today, I'll marry my soulmate." *Lady Caroline or not.*

With her handsome cowboy preacher by her side, and with God's help, she could handle whatever the good Lord had planned for them next.

THE END

Author's Notes

I'd been wanting to write a British cowboy story because my grandfather, Lloyd Earl Fancett, Sr., was the son of English immigrants and he'd worked as a cowboy out west after his first wife died. I recently found my grandfather's misspelled name, too, on a census list of people living on a ranch in South Dakota. Like my hero, Barden, he had light gray eyes. I wrote this story as a nod to my grandfather, who I never knew. He'd died while my poor dad was away fighting in WWII, my grandfather having been hit by a drunk driver and then dying at a hospital some days later. My grandfather reportedly had a fondness for the west, and my two uncles moved to Wyoming as young men and lived out their lives there. By the way, many Englishmen were, indeed, ranchers out west during this time—and there are books that even cover that topic.

Mackinac Island US Army transfers for wounded soldiers in the West to return to Fort Mackinac for light duty happened near the time of this story. Much appreciation to Phil Porter, former Mackinac Island Parks Director, now retired, for his input about the soldiers traveling to Mackinac Island. I was delighted to include my Mackinac bound characters, one who appears in later books.

Acknowledgments

Every story I write is for God, and I thank Him for His many blessings. Thank you to my family for their support, too, for my writing ministry. My dear friend, Cheryl Baranski, now deceased, blessed me by brainstorming this original project with me early on. Also, thank you to Kathleen L. Maher, my former critique partner, who has been such a blessing. Grateful for Regina Fujitani, my professional beta reader for this project, who is also now resides in heaven.

I borrowed many names for this story, as I often do, with permission. My friend, author Melissa Henderson, appears with her husband, Alan. Reader Caryl Kane's name was morphed into a more historically correct Caroline Kane for my heroine. Chris Granville, one of my readers, is the source of the Granville name. Joel Martinchek was a classmate who lived in my neighborhood. Cheatham was borrowed from Cheatham Annex here in Virginia, which is a military installation and not an aristocrat's estate!

Thank you to my 2025 promo team members and advance readers: Melissa Main my critique partner who is also an editor, Alyssa Amey Madeski who also kindly created book graphics, Carolyn Moon Bryant, Evelyn Foreman, Rebecca Tellez, Linda Matson Thomas, Mary Winzenburg, Sherry Moe, Ivy Sterling Lasley, Mary Steinbrenner and Tina Stuck. Thank you to Early Reader Trudy Cordle who is also an editor/proofreader!

A group hug to the Pagels' Pals! This group supports my writing ministry. Thank you also to Avid Christian Fiction Readers, especially Administrator Martha Artyomenko Hurley and founder Tricia Goyer, for all you do. Several of my new readers for the re-release project came from this wonderful group!

Mackinac Island Romances Series

<u>Main titles</u>

Novellas*:*

    Mercy in a Red Cloak - Origin story

    In Desperate Straits - Prequel

Novels:

    My Heart Belongs on Mackinac Island

    Anchored at Mackinac

    Mackinac Island Beacon

<u>Associated books</u>

Novels:

    Behind Love's Wall

Novellas:

    Dime Novel Suitor

    The Sugarplum Ladies

    The Substitute Bride

Bio

CARRIE FANCETT PAGELS, Ph.D. is a multi-award-winning and bestselling Christian fiction author of over twenty-five books. She loves a good cup of tea and keeps her tea cart well stocked! A former psychologist of over twenty-seven years, Carrie was raised in Michigan's beautiful Eastern Upper Peninsula.

You can find Carrie online at Instagram, Facebook, Pinterest, her website www.carriefancettpagels.com, LinkedIn, and on YouTube (with videos of Carrie reading parts of her books).

If you enjoyed this novel,

a review is always

very much appreciated!!!